MW00848577

FANTASY

Published by Sidebrow Books
P.O. Box 86921
Portland, OR 97286
sidebrow@sidebrow.net
www.sidebrow.net

Cover art by Sojourner Truth Parsons
Book design by Jason Snyder

ISBN: 1-940090-11-3
ISBN-13: 978-1-940090-11-5

FIRST EDITION | FIRST PRINTING
9 8 7 6 5 4 3 2 1
SIDEBROW BOOKS 022
PRINTED IN THE UNITED STATES

Sidebrow Books titles are distributed by
Small Press Distribution

Titles are available directly from Sidebrow at
www.sidebrow.net/books

A Member of

www.theintersection.org

Sidebrow is a member of the Intersection Incubator, a program of
Intersection for the Arts (www.theintersection.org) providing fiscal
sponsorship, incubation, and consulting for artists. Contributions
to Sidebrow are tax-deductible to the extent allowed by law.

FANTASY

KIM-ANH SCHREIBER

SIDEBROW BOOKS • 2020 • PORTLAND & SAN FRANCISCO

"Down below there is no exit. Yet neither is there a dead end. Instead I see breaking waves, white foam shimmering in the twilight and my own uncanny reflection. There is no wall at the end of the passage reminding us of the wreckage of the past, but a reflective glass, a screen for transient beauty, a profane illumination."

—Svetlana Boym, *The Future of Nostalgia*

For my grandparents, and my father, and my brother, and my favorite aunts: who made my future shine bright.

COLD OPEN

The first time Ông and Bà went back to Vietnam I was 10 years old. It had been twenty years since they'd left and the United States had just lifted its trade embargo. They were gone for three weeks and when they came home we sat on the floor of their bedroom as they took packages out of their luggage one by one, everything stuffed into large Ziploc bags: photos, heirlooms, documents, things left behind that someone, someone I had never met, had saved for them. I sat in my favorite aunt's lap and we pored over the photos for hours. At one point my mom found her birth certificate and said, shocked, "I'm thirty. I'm not thirty-one—I'm thirty!"

My mom and my aunt laughed wildly. I laughed too, because I would do everything they'd do.

At the time, I thought we were laughing because my grandparents had had so many children that they'd forgotten how old they all were. Only later did I realize that my mom's age was wrong due to a Vietnamese system that begins life at conception rather than birth. In fact, the longer I sit with this scene, the more I realize that it continues to become fleshed out with the things I now know. The story grows as I grow.

I didn't realize, for example, the significance of that trip. I knew where they had come from, and I knew how they had fled, but I did not necessarily understand that they couldn't go back, or that they were living in exile because at the time I had no idea what exile meant, and in a sense when we were together we were always in Vietnam, or more accurately, "Vietnam," an idea filtered through memory, language, and atmosphere: food, smell, and music. I did not know that I was born during the first major waves of Vietnamese immigration, that the shopping centers in the enclaves we frequented were still being built, nor did I know that I would look back and think that that era was the height of a certain formation of Vietnamese-Americanness, a moment which straddled the line between memories of Vietnam being near and far, new identities and sensibilities departing and arriving, when families had multiple generations reflecting multiple forms of assimilation. When we all lived together. I did not know that we were referred to as "New Americans." Being born in America, and raised in America, I did not feel new, and my world was complete. I did not realize until much later that I had spent my whole life making one world out of many different pieces.

I don't remember anything in those Ziploc bags either: none of the photos, heirlooms, or documents. All I remember is laughter: wild and free. Maybe I had once made up a fantasy memory, that after a while became a real memory. That happens a lot. In a way, memory is an evocative curator: Are the individual images all that important, or do they blur into a utopia of the past? All that is important, my memory seems to decide, is that there were tangible memories, documents of identity, and physical inheritances that had been lost and were now restored. I wonder what that restoration feels like: Is it like old software on a new computer? Or is it like hearing a song you used to love and have forgotten, when rediscovery feels just as good as discovery? I cannot know the experience of my grandmother, because we did not share a language of adequate complexity or nuance to describe it. But even if we did, as I do with my mother and aunt, what extraordinary effort would it take to expand and elasticize language to communicate from one person to another what has been lost and found?

I've never encountered anything that was in those plastic bags again. No one has ever shown me an object and said, "This came back from Vietnam." I've heard stories, but I haven't seen a single image of my mother as a child, nor my grandmother, nor any image of any former house. The scene from that day has become a device I return to when I want to think about the material of my inheritance: gestures I copied without understanding why, a longing for joy and laughter as a release. Images, which don't reference what's preserved on their surfaces, but evasive gleaners or ghosts, leading me towards walls, revelations, or refuges. In my imagination I pore over each faded, fading document. They become sites for my own animation, which always reflect "me" more than "what really happened," "what was really on the images," or "what they remember which I never saw," which is not my story to tell, and which, frankly, would be impossible. I was only a child, and in terms of this story, am always the child.

RULES OF STYLE

The 1977 Japanese film *House* begins with Gorgeous posing, wrapped in a sheet, surrounded by candles. The sheet is a palimpsest. Her best friend, Fantasy, holding a camera, is disarmed.

"It's hot," says Gorgeous, in an echoey voice. "Hurry!"

Fantasy takes several pictures.

With each shot, the light changes, the atmosphere changes, and Gorgeous changes, like a mood ring. When the photo shoot's over, she removes her sheet and becomes a teen again. She blows out the candles. The "set" disappears into a science lab.

What Fantasy sees is hidden from the viewer. What her face expresses is illegible, regarding the strange and inexplicable, wearing the most ambient expression as if she's been crossed by a ghost.

"Fantasy," asks Gorgeous. "Why were you staring at me?"

"Because you looked like a witch in a horror movie!"

The girls explode into laughter.

When I first saw *House*, directed by Nobuhiko Obayashi, I had spent the previous months recovering from a bicycle accident in which, running a stop sign to make a left turn, a car clipped me and my bike, sending me flying over the handlebars. I landed on my left hip, twisting my back at the sacral joint, the tailbone, before the car sped away.

At first, maybe because of adrenaline screaming through my body, I didn't feel much at all. I would spin a long, noir-ish story describing the events of that evening, whenever anyone would ask me if I was doing okay, which was my way of saying that I *was* okay. But then, my body began to feel things: low levels of all-over pain and panic. I went to the doctor and was asked—as I was asked over the next two and a half years of medical treatment—to quantify my level of pain. And even though my pain was always changing in character and intensity, my number was always consistent: 3 or 4, as though my body had psychological shelters to shield against pain, as though I could always imagine worse. I was told that young people often say 3 or 4, and this has to do with a high tolerance for pain, and a certain illiteracy in its presence. When you really think about it, many different somatic intensities fall under the umbrella of what we call "pain." Pain is an abstraction: It can be dull, sharp, throbbing, stinging, pounding, or smarting. Pain can be shallow or deep, soft or hard. It can throb, burn, itch, or chafe. I believe it would be best translated through onomatopoeia, so that the speaker and the listener may have a common visceral experience. And then there is psychic pain, and what happens when it intermingles with physical pain, when it's felt in the body, or when it slows the body down and stalls the immune system. Contrary to the language I was given (and asked to use) to describe my pain, the type I felt could not be pointed to and said, "It's here."

I was recommended a lawyer, who set me up with a chiropractor. I went because I did not know how to navigate my own health insurance, didn't understand what it covered in this particular situation, and I couldn't afford for it to not cover everything, and my lawyer said he would pay for all of it, no questions asked. After taking some X-rays, the chiropractor said bluntly, "Your spine is injured. Look—," he gripped a model of the spine and demonstrated how my vertebrae would grind against one another over time: twisting and grinding, twisting and grinding again. The more I was asked to pay attention to it, the more my lower back throbbed, until the pain shot through my shoulders and toes. "The vertebrae allow the passage of the spinal cord from the medulla oblongata to the base of the lumbar region," he demonstrated. "Nerve endings travel outward from the brain, through the spinal cord, to the various areas of the body, like a communication highway. When you have a spinal injury, nerves can be damaged, breaking down the communication highway, making it harder to get vital messages to your organs, making it easier for your organs to break down. See what I mean? *Your spine is the seat of your soul.*"

My heart raced when the chiropractor asked me to describe the pain, and my back flared when asked to locate it. Did my communication highway also break down in this accident? I wondered. The stress of this initial intake session would come to operate as an amplifying technology, causing my back to spasm from the tension produced by the suggestion that my body was changed forever and that I would always be injured, that I was no longer in charge, that, contrary to the idea of my body I previously had, in which it was an ecosystem harmoniously housing the joint, the joint seemed to be destroying the ecosystem. Was my body like a row of dominoes, just waiting for a piece to fall? In a way, this initial intake session sent my injury on a years-long course of recovery in which pain sparked from psychic stress amplified my injury and thus became "real."

The chiropractor promised he would make me better. I laid down with my head in a little hole and he cracked my back. He remarked, "It makes sense that you're experiencing panic right now. The impact might have unlocked stress your spine has stored for a very long time.

"You know," he mused, "the spine remembers everything."

Pain, I found, disrupted the illusory continuity of my body, which I had previously seen as both separate from the world and separate from my mind. After the accident, that all changed, because my injury was emotional and my pain was as much ambient as locatable. Soon I began to see my spine in everyday objects: in a vape, in an ice cube tray, in a 2 x 4 piece of wood, in iPad display stands. Around the same time, news reports began surfacing of refugees arriving in boats on the shores of Greek islands. I read them obsessively, in my bed. My body was still, unmoving, but I saw my spine as a boat. A carrier of memories across time. And I saw my memories like I saw my spine: fractured, but unlocked; in need of, as my physical therapist would say, "articulation."

And so when I first watched *House*, I saw my spine in every cut and seam—a communication highway. That which connects disparate shots and scenes to create an illusion of continuity. The biggest privilege of inhabiting a body, I learned, was to not even notice it was being inhabited. To fit perfectly inside the home one is confined to: your world.

In that first scene of *House*, Fantasy takes Gorgeous's picture in a square frame nested within a standard rectangular frame. At one minute and twenty seconds, after removing her sheet, Gorgeous fluffs her hair and falls backwards, "clicking into" the background frame, as if the background frame has been waiting for the foreground frame to catch up to it. Suddenly the two separate, overlaid shots cohere into one. Watching that shot, I thought: That is what I want for my body. That is what I want for my memories. I felt that in watching *House*, in watching its unreality and discontinuity, I was seeing something fundamentally true. Something my spine remembered. But what?

I watched the version of *House* translated and distributed by Criterion Collection, which describes the film as a "hallucinatory head trip about a schoolgirl who travels with six classmates to her ailing aunt's creaky country home and comes face-to-face with evil spirits, a demonic house cat, a bloodthirsty piano, and other ghoulish visions… Equally absurd and nightmarish, *House* might have been beamed to Earth from some other planet." I'd summarize the basic plot structure as: Following her father's announcement that he is remarrying, Gorgeous and her friends—Sweet, Melody, Prof, Fantasy, Mac, and Kung Fu—head to her mother's childhood home for the summer, where they are hunted and eaten alive by her aunt's cannibalistic ghost, who, still waiting for her fiancé to return from the war, consumes all of the unmarried girls who come to visit her.

As the film's lore goes, the film company Toho, noted for producing and distributing the films of Akira Kurosawa as well as the *Godzilla* franchise, approached Obayashi, a successful TV commercial director and experimental filmmaker, and suggested he write a film that could be a "Japanese version of *Jaws*"—which, as I see it, could mean any number of things: A summer box office hit. Teeth in the water. A monster under a surface designed to provoke delight. The ocean as void, as appetite, as shape-shifting substance that spreads and seeps into every surface available to it. But to conceive of *his* Japanese version of *Jaws*, Obayashi asked his preadolescent daughter Chigumi what would make a good scary movie. Sitting at the mirror brushing her hair, she answered, "If my reflection… could jump out of the mirror and eat me."

This iconic scene—the cannibalistic reflection, the girl brushing her hair—is replicated in the film and foundational to its lore, at least in the English language press surrounding the film's rerelease by Janus Films and Criterion Collection in 2010. This repetition might be because this mirror scene is at the inception of the film's imagistic universe or because of the limitations of myth, marketing, or memory. Also foundational to the film's lore is Nobuhiko Obayashi's childhood: Born in Onomichi, a city located near Hiroshima Prefecture, in 1938, Obayashi has said that when the atomic bomb dropped on Hiroshima in 1945, all of his close childhood friends died. His overall creative project, it could be inferred, is to convey the experience of war in service of a message for peace, to a generation who grew up in a period of peace, because peace, Obayashi has said, came from the pleasure of forgetting. He has called *House* "a fantasy with the atomic bomb as a theme." In the retrospective making-of documentary *Constructing a House*, he has called the "exaggerated and beautiful world of fantasy" "our generation's version of a horror film."

Imdb.com credits the writing of the *House* screenplay to Chiho Katsura, and Chigumi Obayashi with the original story. By the time Obayashi approached Katsura, he and Chigumi had already sketched out the moments in which the house attacks the girls—futons drop on Sweet; Fantasy fishes Mac's head out of the well; a mirror swallows Gorgeous; and so on—as well as all of the characters' names: Gorgeous, Fantasy, Mac, Kung Fu, Sweet, Melody, and Prof. According to his interview in *Constructing a House*, Katsura drew from Walter de la Mare's story "The Riddle," in which an old woman lives alone in her house and is visited by seven grandchildren who disappear into a wooden chest. He wrote the script and handed it to Obayashi, who added his own narrative about a house haunted by the spirit of a woman waiting for her lover to return from the war. Katsura never saw the script again until it was done. He wondered if such an absurd story would ever get made.

While Katsura can be seen as the one tasked with sketching the blueprint for the house that is *House*, Obayashi speaks of he and Chigumi as having "written the film together." This creative process seems to replicate the doubling that occurs in the film between Gorgeous and her cannibalistic aunt, and can tell us something about the anxieties of both creators simultaneously: They both saw a monster in their own reflection, but each monster-and-reflection was entirely unique, and at the same time, a reflection of the other's monster-and-reflection, as if one generation's monster pollinates the next generation's monster like a seed. It provides a great tactic for approaching an impossible problem: to draw a picture. "If the topic was movie stories and characters," Chigumi recounts in *Constructing a House*, "we could understand each other despite the generation gap." And so, if Nobuhiko saw horror imbued in the veneer of fantasy, then what did Chigumi, and "the generation who grew up in peace," the generation that made *House* a box office success and cult classic, see? Understand that I am treating Nobuhiko and Chigumi Obayashi as characters of my own, overloading their words with meaning in order to reach across my own generation gap, to meet my mother in the mirror, knowing that I could never tell their story of what really happened and what they saw, because, as I've said, that's impossible. The story is entirely mine.

For three years I busied myself with research. I watched more Obayashi films, including his 1990 documentary *Making of Dreams: A Movie Conversation Between Akira Kurosawa and Nobuhiko Obayashi*, where Kurosawa wonders aloud, "Where does the film come alive?" I read Obayashi's descriptions of war. I read about the film's production and publicity, and its soundtrack. I watched *House* on silent, with the subtitles on, playing many different kinds of music in the background. I watched *Jaws*, *The Wizard of Oz*, *Snow White*, *Blood and Roses*, kung fu films, and other films I suspected *House* paid homage to in some way. I watched *Godzilla*, and read about the similarity between Godzilla's skin texture and the keloid scars found on survivors of the bombings. I read about how some audiences called *Godzilla* "grotesque junk," but that others identified with the creature, seeing it as a nuclear refugee, made immortal and powerful and turning its aggression against those who manifested it. I read about how some saw the creature as a representation of the past, and a way of incorporating the past into the future. I read about the relationship between the living and the dead. I read about monsters, and ghosts, and cannibals, and cannibalistic ghosts. I read about camp, cuteness, cheesiness, and "cruel optimism," read *The Riddle*, *The Yellow Wallpaper*, *Great Expectations*, and watched an entire archive of films and TV shows about groups of women trapped in houses: *Mekong Hotel*, *Keeping Up with the Kardashians*, *Pretty Little Liars*, *The Virgin Suicides*. I read about unruly women. I read about melodrama, and the maternal gaze of the soap opera spectator. I read about the solicitation of female shoppers, the strategic placement of mirrors in public places, consumerism, and citizenship. I examined Criterion's translation, to the best of my ability, and wrote down my questions. I sent them out to be answered. I never heard back. I read about modernism, and postmodernism. I read about the Tokyo avant-garde in the sixties, Butoh, Manga, and Japanese fashion, and theories about these cultural phenomena and their relationship to the atomic bomb. I jotted notes on intergenerational trauma from a variety of sources: "Secondary traumatization is the phenomenon of direct or indirect traumatization of children via epigenetics or their parents' post-traumatic symptoms, such as dissociation in the face of attachment or the desire to maintain control. Very often the unexplainable or inexpressible or inconceivable is recognized by the next generation as an affective sensitivity or a chaotic urgency, ambient anxiety that children can sense but not understand, through messages, gestures, values, thought systems, and stories, a code that is being communicated without translation. Children of 'survivors' are often implicitly tasked with representing without 're-experiencing,' tasked to be tour guides through an untold past." I read a blog post about *House*'s queerness: "It's queer in its atmosphere, and its narrative margins." I read about feminized illnesses concerning eating and agoraphobia. I thought about the relationship between the consumption of food and the consumption of things. I read a chapter called "Imaging Modern Girls in the Japanese Woman's Film," in which it was written that "the subtle deployment of the modern girl in popular culture exhibits the complex interplay of modernity and national identity operating at all levels of Japanese cinema." I also read a chapter called "Adaptation as 'Transcultural Mimesis' in Japanese Cinema," in which its author wrote that "Japanese filmmakers were engaged in a practice of transcultural mimesis that aimed, simultaneously, at *re-creating* Hollywood film in Japan, *parodying* the absurdities of American cinema (e.g., heterosexual romance, strong female characters) in the Japanese context, and even *learning* from the gap between Japanese and American cinema something of the invisible but nonetheless real 'geopolitical incline' between Japan and the United States."

I read many, many descriptions of *House*, just to get a handle on what people said about it. Some called the film "wild," "visionary pudding," with "nothing to say about it," that it's "quite fun," "pure, horrific fun," "you know it will be fun," "fast and fun," "so much fun," "like a nightmarish version of *Pee-wee's Playhouse*" that's "eye-poppingly demented," and so on. *Little White Lies* called *House* both "one of the most 'terrible' films ever made" and "hugely entertaining." *AV Club* wrote about its "sublime, nearly indescribable fucked-uptitude," which made watching the film like "a rush chasing a rush," "like jamming fistfuls of delicious candy into your mouth for 90 minutes," "set to a disconcerting pop score that's like the aural equivalent of shag carpeting." *The Village Voice* wrote that "it may be impossible not to be stunned into dumbness by Nobuhiko Obayashi's *Hausu* (*House*)," while *The New York Times* writes that "it's easy to track the plot points in 'House' and rather more difficult to grasp why Mr. Obayashi tells the story the way he does." And while almost everything I read expressed a sense of sheer bafflement, I believed that these descriptions mirrored if not were deliberately aware of the visceral violence *House*'s form evoked. *Little White Lies* wrote that "it dissects itself, makes all its seams visible." *AV Club* wrote that "it's like he's slashing his canvas at the same time he's painting it." *The Village Voice* wrote that the girls "start getting minced up, one by one, into crude superimpositions, perambulating body parts, and rivers of blood that look like cherry Hi-C." "This juxtaposition of girlish glee with unexplainable, gory phenomena," *The Black List* wrote, "ends up commenting on the ways we craft female narratives and female characters throughout the entire genre of horror."

"The film's biggest trick, however, might be convincing the audience that it is *not* scary," declared *The McGill Tribune*. "Though it seems innocent and even childish at first, underneath *Hausu*'s campy veneer lies an extremely sinister film. When Gorgeous, Melody, Kung-Fu, Prof, and Fantasy finally decide to call the police after losing their other friends, the camera's over-exposure gives the image a ghostly quality. Gorgeous—now possessed—picks up the phone, and, from the other side of the line, come the grueling, horrid screams of her friends. These kinds of eerie moments are rare, but they suggest a much darker film below the superficial playfulness. The darker scenes are haunting within a movie where, for the most part, its characters implausibly ignore the horrors going on around them, and in which scares are often played off as jokes. The film toes the line between comedic and horrifying: In a running gag, characters yell 'An illusion!' whenever they encounter the supernatural. *Hausu* doesn't take itself too seriously, but it's no less scary for it." And then, scrolling through the variety of freewheeling descriptions, each trying to match the formal innovation and iconoclastic aesthetic of the film, I found this one, in a video essay uploaded by Kogonada: "The film has two halves. The first half establishes the lightness of the new generation after the bomb... the second half of the film is primarily dedicated to the nonsensical destruction of the girls. If we were to find the exact center of this film, we would land on what I consider to be the most significant and telling scene. We see a convergence of identities played out in the mirrors: between two generations, between the past and the present, between the dead and the living."

With so much information, my essay on *House* expanded and contracted like an accordion. I spent so long in front of the computer, reading and writing, that I absorbed the film's energy: I felt that my own body, my own past, and my own walls were swallowing me, and I encountered this feeling with a strange familiarity, a cozy claustrophobia. My findings were interesting but they seemed to be missing the point, and anyway, who did I think I was, a Japanese cinema scholar? Each fact I encountered seemed no more important than any other, or opened a door to a room that led to more rooms, that led to more rooms, to infinity, and in every room I only learned how much I didn't know, and could not know from such a distance. I was a terrible translator, and I doubted the weird objectivity of translation. The meaning of *House*, actually, didn't seem much different than the house itself, swallowing every fresh fact that entered its orbit, digesting and regurgitating it back up into its soupy logic. Throughout it all, what seemed significant was a particular doubling between me and Chigumi. I kept thinking about that day my grandparents came home from their first trip back to Vietnam, after the Clinton administration had lifted the trade embargo, when we sat on their floor and looked at photographs. I was ten years old, like Chigumi, and it had been twenty years since the fall of Saigon. A similar amount of time had passed between the dropping of the atomic bomb on Hiroshima and the writing of *House*, and I think our "images," whatever is imprinted onto them, reflect two generations processing one distant event in the particular moment in time in which they occur: a generation later, in a space that had been leveled in a war, in a reconstruction sown by death, radiation, industrialism, hyperproduction, globalism, the solidifying power of the state, and the new, unfamiliar landscape of home.

To enforce some type of order into an otherwise chaotic system of messages, I chose to interpret the film through the recurring appearance of the DISFIGURED FACE. Of course, no real faces were disfigured in *House*'s production. Having cut his teeth first in the avant-garde cinema scene, and then in the commercial industry, Obayashi was a master of special effects, which were realized entirely on set or in camera through mattes, animation, or collage. His desired result was to depict "the effect of special effects," as if a child had created them, to simulate or gesture toward horror without really depicting it. In other words, *House* isn't scary and its special effects don't serve a conventional idea of filmic realism, which typically allows the viewer to forget that they are watching a film at all. Special effects, in this case, expose the reality of making a film and operate like a mask, like a disfigured face on the surface of the story, but instead of appearing natural, deceiving the viewer in its masquerade, the viewer becomes ever more aware that the *face*, the central organ of sense and primary emotional expresser, is also the *surface*, used for presentation and connection, and perhaps just a *façade*, merely an outward appearance that hides or belies its interior. Anything that presents itself as a site of relation can have a face, or a façade, including a person, clock, wall, or building, performing an aesthetic argument, a style, and the manic sheen of good times.

The word *face* also acts as a verb, a method of positioning toward someone or something, as well as the act of confronting or adjusting to something. A wall might face you, or you might turn to face the wall. A wall might have ears, eyes, or pictures, or the wall might open up to be a window. The wall might be jagged or crooked in texture; there might be a lot going on under the surface, even if everything feels light, and white. To admonish yourself, you might turn yourself in toward the wall.

A person (I, you) can disfigure; a thing (a bomb) can disfigure; and an abstraction can disfigure (time, the past). The word disfigurement often requires violent terms to define it, such as impair, soil, or damage. It originates in the Latin *figura*, or "shape, figure, or form." With the prefix *dis-* indicating reversal, negation, removal, or release, the term implies that the action destroys a unity-which-can-no-longer-be, a "control," an ideal from which one has been removed and to where one can no longer return. Another word for disfigure could be *deface*.

A face can be read (through expressions) or be written (with makeup), and in this way has some relationship to interior life. But if it does not mirror interiority, if it becomes a *façade*, the face shifts into a mask. Sometimes masks, makeup, expressions, and scars can create a new face, a face with a shadow of the past, that is, from somewhere within, *speaking.*

Disfigurement was embedded in Obayashi's desires for production and reception, which he has described as "very chaotic." For *House*, he worked mostly with non-actors and shot without a storyboard. He would wear ridiculous outfits, race, skip, or play games with the actresses. Dissatisfied with their performances, he would play the film's soundtrack, which changed the spirit of their acting. When the music played in a minor chord, the actors played sad. When it played in a major chord, they played happy. The crew reported that the shoot reminded them why they loved movies, but that they had no idea what the film would eventually look like. Obayashi reported that the special effects did not always turn out how he had intended. Critics complained about the girls' acting, that they always looked like they were dancing. Obayashi said that he found that the teenagers of that era, his actresses, could access their emotions through rhythm more fluently than language. "I create this whole chaotic monster and give it to the audience with no explanation and no clarity," he has remarked. "I call it a 'charming chaos.'… I want them to find their own way and get them lost first and have them find their own way back."

"Cinematic realism," according to Obayashi's definition of it, could be the camera shaking in the hands of its operator. It could be a cut into the film and the collaging of other layers over it, or a matte placed over the lens so that only the frame-within-the-frame is captured and recorded. It could be a mural of the sky, in place of the sky. Anything that reveals the hand of the maker and the "reality of make-believe." *House* is no more "artificial" than any other film or any cultural narrative or construct, Obayashi argues through *Making of Dreams*, by focusing much of the viewer's attention towards the extraordinary effort put into the appearance of naturalism, long scenes gazing on set painters painting a "glow in the morning light" on ordinary wheat stalks. But this has long been the task of post-modernists and the avant-garde: to denaturalize the "natural," "real," "continuous" story, when there is none.

I use this concept of realism to understand mine — that feeling of overall continuity despite persistent cultural discontinuity, a mutant feeling that comes from growing up in two families from two different countries with two different wars hovering in the background of our lives in America. There is no story, no history, and no experience without gaps that flare and destruct their body. Every seam I encountered in the fabric of my reality was like a disfigurement that someone had smoothed over and left silent, so that whatever world I "clicked into" did not click into a shared world, did not contain my past, so that I was told that my reality was not real.

As with pain, I don't know where my memory resides, what it produces, or what it looks like. Being born in the mid-eighties, I remember my childhood through the bright light of Kodak film and the washed-out palette of videotape, which degrades as it fades into the past. But this isn't memory — it's aesthetics, and the emotional response I project onto it. I like to imagine that Obayashi also used layers of film and "effect" to get closer to a kind of emotional memory impossible to depict, and this brings me closer to my mother's exile, and my exile from my mother, the "breaking away" we both did in the intergenerational chain link of emotional life. When I was a child she left home and moved very far away. I would see her every other weekend, and for one month in the summer. In her absence, anything else that could operate as a mother-force rushed in to fill up the space of the empty, emptying, emptiness. It is a space I don't know the bounds of, that spreads and seeps into every surface available to it, as immediate and as imperceptible as the interior of the embryonic body.

And how can I be my mother's daughter if I don't have her face?

Her disfigurement?

What is more figurative than the frame?

In total I counted 37 unique occurrences of the disfigured face in *House*, and separated them into eight categories: dislocation; through the window; through a shroud; through animation or scrawling over (extradiegetic); through cross-fade; through broken mirrors; by fire (extradiegetic); by water or disturbing the water. I chose to talk about this house—my house— through this image because I do not have the language to talk about the haunting. Because my own images have faded. I chose to talk about the disfigured face as a way to talk about my disfigured spine, because I do not have the language to describe its memories. I have attempted to reconstruct her story—my mother's story—through many of the same methods: encounter a reflection, face it, and deface it. Make something monstrous, and play. Comprehend what I saw as a child. These disfigurements, marks across a surface, cohere into a code as an aesthetic of reassembly. They are all I have, and I care for them. It is a maternal gesture I give to her. And I give to myself.

ANATOMY OF A CRITICAL INCIDENT

It was a very strange, sad time when my grandfather Opi, my father's father, first told me about "Anatomy of a Critical Incident." I had just injured my back, and he had just had a stroke, though he didn't know I had injured my back, because I didn't want to stress him out. He had confided to me, on my first day visiting him, that he thought that the stroke was due to high blood pressure, to stress he had bottled up for his entire life, a bodily memory of various forms of imprisonment in his youth. For years, he told me, stress would rise up in his dreams: dreams about the camps. "I dream a feeling of panic," he told me. "I dream I'm losing control and will be beaten for it. For things like not gathering enough straw."

My grandparents were always storytellers; they were never silent about their past. They reminisced constantly, mostly at meals. Over plates of cheese and meat my grandmother would talk about running away to Berlin, to dance for the Staatsoper Unter Den Linden. Spreading liverwurst over bread she would tell me about her childhood in a bombed Dresden, about meeting my grandfather at a typewriter factory, about smuggling news over the border between east and west, about fleeing East Berlin. Over tea cups filled with coffee and milk my grandfather would talk about their first weeks in the West Berlin refugee camps, how his mother was depressed and he went to the local college, and they said that he couldn't register for two more years because of his status. "I said to them, I grew up in Hitler's Germany for twelve years," he'd recall. "Then I was in Stalin's camps for six years. Now you tell me two more years. I have spent more than half of my life in prison. Please—let me begin my life!" Over passed bread baskets my grandfather would detail the experience of biking home at the end of the war, to wish his mother a happy birthday, a day when he thought he would die, tanks rumbling in the distance, a gas mask hanging off his handles. Except, after he wished her a happy birthday, after she said, "I named you Peter because you are a rock, you are a stone upon which to build, you shall not change, though others around you might change," the war ended.

As if touched by divine benevolence, I would imagine. I had attended the local Catholic school, where teachers referred to Europe as the "old world," and each year during Lent we would watch film reenactments of Jesus's hands being nailed to the cross. When they lifted up that giant cross, as big as a tree, with Jesus attached to it, he would groan and cast his eyes to the Heavens in Agony. Then I would go home, filled with fear. "Daddy, can I be crucified?" I asked, my head filling up with new ways to die. My father, a non-believer, who had sent me there thinking God or nuns could be a form of support in my mother's absence, told me no—crucifixion only happened in the old days. "The Bible is FICTION," he assured me, but somewhere in my oozy child-brain the sufferings of Christ and the sufferings of my grandparents met in the same pan Old World, a hybrid European/Middle Eastern/Medieval/Victorian hillside, bathed in the same holy light, the light that touched all fiction. Like Jesus, my grandfather had suffered and lived many lives so that he could bring thine grace to thee. Or something like that—the stuff of legends and myths in the manger in which I was born. For the first grade Christmas play, I drew the role of The Star out of a hat. I wore an old ghost Halloween costume onto which my grandmother Omi had glued an entire package of gold star stickers and I danced across the stage, leading the three shepherds, one carrying gold, one carrying frankincense, and one carrying myrrh, to the child who, sort of like me, I thought while wiggling my star-stickered fingertips, had been born after a long, exhausting journey on the back of a donkey, after knocking over and over again on hotel doors in Bethlehem, hearing again and again, "There is no room at the inn. There is no room at the inn. There is no room at the inn."

Not only was I the only one in my class whose parents were not American, the only one whose parents were divorced, and the only one whose mom was always half an hour late every other Friday when she came to pick me up in the car line, I was also among the non-baptized, and without the sacraments I could not receive grace. And so, because I bore these special shames, I had to form my own relationship with Jesus, my own communion. I was helped by the fact that my grandparents lived in Bethlehem, Pennsylvania, and that I had been born in a town called Zionsville, Pennsylvania, in the suburbs of Philadelphia, the birthplace of America, home of the Liberty Bell and the Betsy Ross house, founded by William Penn as a haven for Quakers suffering from religious persecution. I held on tight to the idea that even though I grew up in a place where there were not many immigrants, the fact that my parents, one German immigrant and one Vietnamese refugee, found each other in these two towns named after holier-seeming places in older-seeming worlds, made sense in the context of Pennsylvania's birth, America's birth, and of course, Jesus's birth. Standing on stage for the rest of the play after I had completed my North Star duties, hands clasped in prayer, the kind where your fingers do not fold into one another but shoot straight up towards the sky, I should not have found much in common with this wood beam lying on a bed of straw, actors moving around it; still I found my heart glowing bright with deep empathy as I pulled its world into mine, casting my eyes to the sky in Agony.

One day, like in a movie, I sat in a chair in prayer while my classmates shuffled past me, knees knocking my knees, to stand in a line to accept the body of Christ and his blood, or whatever that stuff was, in that giant chalice the size of a head, like God-blessed little lambs. I realized that this situation was familiar too, in a very different way: Whatever these kids knew, whatever rituals they encountered on Sundays, I would experience only as a visitor, relegated to the role of the one watching. Maybe instead of stories of war, they bent their heads to hear the exact same prayer murmured over the exact same baskets of bread—definitely not rye bread from the German butcher, the one Omi frequented every week. I was outside of that experience. I would always be near, but I would never drink the cup. I could never taste the body. Staring at the choir singing the ecstatic song "Pentacle of the Sun," which I had always misheard as "Tentacles of the Sun," where the sopranos shout, "and sing, sing to the glory of the Lord!" I had a vision from my station in the plastic chair, amongst the uninvited and uninitiated. A secret power in what I saw: the knowledge of my father against the knowledge of the world. It's all FICTION, I thought, smiling sublimely as God dissolved into a golden, tentacled octopus in the sky. For some feelings wash over you with such polyphonic force a whole chorus must open their mouths to express it.

It was easy for me to forsake God because God was as solid as a Nintendo game console or an Egg McMuffin, shimmering enchantments that adorned life and made it less ordinary, but could also be easily tossed in the trash, or left behind as we moved from one house to another, or not needed on a given day. The older I became, the more my childhood experience of religion appeared as an accoutrement of another time. If my family had believed, that might have felt different. It might have felt like a house with no exit and no windows, with no way to imagine the outside. But they didn't believe. My father's family had never set foot in any kind of religious institution, and my mother's family were all Buddhists. Occasionally my mom took me to temple and I sat on a pillow while everyone else seemed to know what to chant and when to prostrate. Mostly, I watched my grandmother light incense at her temple above her TV, chant, and meditate every single day. But I wasn't invited into that activity, either. Nobody explained what was happening.

My era as a young zealot was a deep cut in my personal past when my grandfather told me about "Anatomy of a Critical Incident" in his attic office on a late afternoon in early summer. Disappearing through an attic door I had never noticed, emerging with a thin yellow pamphlet, he told me that he and my father had written the pamphlet, that it was a theory of accidents, operator error, and alarms. "A hole in a walkway represents a hazard because a person may fall into the hole and become injured," it began. "The best safety measure is obviously to either close the hole or cover the hole, which would prevent an accident completely. Under certain circumstances, this may not be possible. As an alternative, the hole may be cushioned with air bags so that no injury occurs if someone should fall into the hole."

When I read "Anatomy of a Critical Incident," I thought that there might be an inherited grammar to the ways we visualize that which is beyond our comprehension. Was my grandfather talking about accidents, his body, or his memory? Suppose he was talking about memory, the rabbit hole of memory, about cushioning the hole with air bags, protecting his fall, and designing intricate systems to prevent the accident completely. Suppose that intricate system is already there, under our noses: stress, the internal alarm, ringing its bell in his dreams. This image is not unlike my anatomy and my stress, though no amount of signs could have prevented my accident in its many forms. And what of my father, the silent author of the text? What was his contribution to this theory that describes, essentially, an intervention?

I had never really been invited into their collaboration—they were engineers, I was not. My mind was daydreaming about different machines, systems, bodies, and incidents. I have wanted to be a writer for most of my life and for most of my life my grandfather has said that if I would learn German we could collaborate on a book, a chronicle of his memories. But I do not speak German, and I do not speak the language of his memories. I can be a dutiful lamb, assistant to his vision, but I'm not; I've chosen to be a bad daughter with my own visions. My language is culled from entirely different roots. He grew up in a tiny town where his family lived on the same tiny road that they had lived on since the twelfth century, and they still live there today, people whom I have never met. When he was born, he had no reason to think that the circumstances of his life would be fated to take him very far away, to another world, and to this day, he still returns to the street where he was born and dreams of the life he could have had, one he envisions through much simpler pleasures. I, on the other hand, was born over shifting sands. What became my life-long investigation was to uncover if many worlds could exist in the same space, if I could hold several truths simultaneously. I don't know if my desire for this type of communion led me to look for meaning in the space between every world I inhabited, or if my desire for meaning constructed the space between.

House begins on the first day of summer. Gorgeous comes home from school, looking forward to a vacation with her father spent at their summer home in Karuiza. Her house is meticulously artificial, adorable, and urbane: Astroturf on the balcony, a painted pink and yellow backdrop for a sky, a tiny putt-putt course, and an egg-shaped swing. A wall of beveled glass tiles divides interior and exterior, and provides a useful texture to disfigure a subject before a camera's eye.

Her father, smoking on the patio and wearing an outfit straight out of *Saturday Night Fever*, surprises her. He's come home early from shooting a movie. He's a film composer: "Better than Morricone," he asserts. She's thrilled, jumping into his arms like a small baby, before he delivers her the terrible news: a new woman, his soon-to-be wife, Ryoka Ema, whose hair catches the wind at just the right angle, who approaches Gorgeous as if floating, oozing an aura of synthetic soap opera stardom, is coming with them. She presents Gorgeous with a white scarf.

"She's going to be your mom," he says.

Behind the distorted glass wall, Gorgeous's face appears to float out of her own face while she repeats after her father... "My mom?"

"It's been eight years since your mother died," he explains. "It's about time we had a home again."

In a rage, she yells: "I won't go with you!" And flings the white scarf into the air. Everything freezes, except for the scarf, fluttering slowly to the ground, unable to catch the wind. Locking herself in her room, Gorgeous picks up a photo of her mom, declaring: "I'm back, Mom!"

"Dad's disappointed us," she whispers, gazing at an old family photo. So she defaces him.

And from here, *House* is set in a world of females, about a world of females, generations of females trapped in a house. There are four types of females in the world of this film:

1. Teenagers
2. Mothers
3. Wives
4. Non-wives

In the world of this film, there are certain unspoken laws to abide by: Teenagers are not mothers, and girls never become women. Instead, they pass through a threshold to another realm and never return, they disappear into voids, they become brides, they become hungry. Disappearing into body parts, lips, hands, heads, and eyeballs, they become just anatomy: organs longing. Wives and non-wives (non-teenage women) often appear with the wind. Teenagers in the still, motionless air.

Dreaming a dreamy dream, Gorgeous lays in bed, looking at photos of the three of them: mother, father, daughter—the nuclear family. Because the same actress, Kimiko Ikegami, played both Gorgeous and her mother, it can be difficult to separate which character is appearing in each image, and that should be thought of as purposeful. The "character" of Gorgeous is stuck in a loop, a possession, which is especially confusing in scenes in which a character appears in a traditional Shinto wedding costume: white kimono, white paper hat, wig, and white face makeup. This bride-ghost that prowls Auntie's house and eats the girls could either be Auntie, Gorgeous, Gorgeous's mother, or a broader, more abstract haunting, since the wedding gown allows these female characters to don a standard wardrobe in which they can lose their identities and inhabit a formless, ambient mass whose face keeps switching. Just like the character of Gorgeous can slip into her mother's body by being played by the same actress, so Auntie will wear her wedding gown—the same gown as her sister's, as every traditional Japanese bride, ostensibly—while eating the unmarried girls who have entered her house. When Gorgeous is eaten, she merges, through tricks of camera, editing, and acting, with her mother and Auntie, prowling the house and leading the girls closer and closer to the death forgotten within the giant house forgotten inside time. And so, the girl becomes a bride becomes an image, becomes ambient, becomes a ghost, becomes a monster, trust-falling into the cult of womanhood. Mothers, the ones who are not alive, are always pursued, becoming motherland, mother tongue. Becoming one another.

Rather than go on vacation with her father and Ryoko Ema, Gorgeous decides to run away, to flee to her aunt's house, whom she has not seen since she was six years old, dragging her six friends with her. "To my mom's hometown!" she says.

The girls venture deep into the maternal ecology, from where we are never to return.

The wind blows.

I never asked for another mother.

The code phrase to evacuate in Operation Frequent Wind was, "The temperature is 105 degrees and rising," and it was broadcast on Armed Forces Radio in Saigon, Vietnam, on April 30, 1975, alongside the song "White Christmas." Chuck Neil, a Saigon-based broadcaster, has written that, contrary to most accounts, the version of "White Christmas" he used was Tennessee Ernie Ford's, not Bing Crosby's. He noted that the song was chosen not because of its historical relevance to World War II, when it was written to remind young soldiers of home, but because it was disruptive: Every American would recognize that it shouldn't be playing in the spring. But "by the time it all came down," he wrote, "every Vietnamese in town must have known what was happening."

That day, an estimated 2,500 evacuees gathered within the U.S. Embassy compound. Another 10,000 surrounded the gates attempting to enter, while helicopters lifted thousands of evacuees from dawn till dusk. Many who should have left, who had been promised evacuation, were left behind in the scramble to leave the country, "gazing skyward in vain," as a columnist once wrote, "for what one survivor called 'the dream in the wind.'" It is said that over $5 million was burned, along with a war's worth of intelligence documents. The tamarind tree in the center of the courtyard was cut down to make a helicopter landing. At 11:30 p.m. the People's Army of Vietnam raised the flag of the National Liberation Front for South Vietnam over the Presidential Palace, now renamed the Reunification Palace.

In the PBS documentary *Last Days in Vietnam*, a witness to the Fall of Saigon recalled years of hearing the *ch-ch-ch* chopper sound in his dreams. He called it "dreaming in the wind."

In my mom's version of the story, my grandfather, Ông, came home that day and told the family to pack one bag to leave. He, a high-ranking government official, would stay behind to take care of some kind of business. My grandmother, Bà, four months pregnant, gathered her eleven children and ran, in a procedure that had been discussed but never rehearsed. Arriving at the U.S. Embassy, my mom, ten years old, was so terrified of the helicopters that she went limp and her brothers dragged her across the concrete, running, and so her shins were skinned when they flew to the cargo ship. I think of that moment as a drag through the fugue, a big line drawn down a little leg demarcating a new life, a new person, a new time. It is a boundary.

To the military personnel shepherding evacuees into helicopters, my grandmother insisted her family leave together. She was told that there were too many of them—twelve—and that they would have to split. She said that she was a mother leaving alone, and if they did not leave together, they would never see each other again. She waited and waited. She and her children were flown together on the last helicopter carrying Vietnamese refugees from the U.S. Embassy during the Fall of Saigon.

Many more people were not so lucky, including my grandfather. The next day, stationed at a predetermined dock, he waited for a helicopter that had been promised but never arrived. I used to wonder about this day, all its minutes I would never know, far more than I would wonder about the Fall of Saigon, for which there was always so much footage for me to watch, scanning the faces for my family, looking for a woman with many, many children, looking for a little girl with skinned knees. I would wonder if the feeling of waiting merged with the gravity of the gray sky, so heavy now that his family was somewhere in it. Even though Saigon is always described as being left in "chaos," I imagine the dock, the air, the plants, the water as silent and still, as if my grandfather were walking around in a photograph. I imagine that he was arrested right there on that dock, waiting, because why turn back now, now that there was no more Saigon, no more family to return to.

The captain of the cargo ship took pity on my mom, her skinned knees. She was allowed to stay in the captain's quarters while the family kept to the cargo compartment. My aunts always joke that up there in the captain's quarters, she ate like a princess while they shared one bowl of rice between them. That's an example, they say, of why she was always the child sent to the market. She is said to have been so beautiful, at such a young age, that she could sail through the five glass security entrances guarding my grandfather's office, and so, by prettiness and ease of access, she is said to have been the child always taken to lunch.

This was the story told over and over again: It was our origin story. While picking pomegranate seeds or kernels of corn off their husks and arranging them in rows that I called trains on a plate, my mother and my aunts repeated the same details: the one bag, the last helicopter, the skinned knees, the baby in the belly. I would imagine that at this moment, shimmering as history gathered them in the palm of its hands and lifted them up to the heavens, my family became gods. The Fall of Saigon was always the door they opened to enter our mythical life. It became my key.

"Chocolate, candy, bread, love, and dreams!" breathes Mac as they board the train. While they ride, Gorgeous tells her friends about Auntie. Her story appears to her friends as an animated wonderland through which they are passing, watching through the window. "A rainbow!" says one. "Over the rainbow!" says another.

"Tell me about your hometown. What's your aunt like?" the girls ask Gorgeous.

"She and my mom loved each other very much," she says wistfully. "My mom took me there once when I was six. I haven't seen her since."

The animated wonderland is interrupted by a shot into a camera lens, and an old newsreel of war planes in the sky. The past looks just like a movie.

"A long time ago," Gorgeous begins, "Japan was in a big war." She tells her friends that Auntie was engaged when her fiancé was drafted to fight in World War II. We see him open his draft card; it turns pink. He promises to return. They kiss, and the image glitches, flickering in and out as we see a mushroom cloud explode over their necking heads, as if the content has overloaded the image. Soldiers march out of the head/cloud. A dissonant chord plays. The girls exclaim, "It's a kiss of fire!"

Auntie's fiancé leaves for the war. He is shot and dies while flying a plane.

The war ends.

He does not come home.

The memory of war is told with the story of forgetting, but Auntie cannot forget. She holds a rose at his grave. The rose cries like a baby with red, scribbly tears, shrivels up, and dies. Five years later, Gorgeous's mother marries. She is photographed in her bridal gown and makeup. White on white on white. Auntie stands sadly behind her sister, holding her cat

Blanche. The camera flash reveals mushroom clouds. The girls gasp: "It's like cotton candy!"

Auntie waits, and waits, and waits, and waits, growing hungrier and hungrier.

Diversion: On my stomach, there's a line stretching from hip to hip. It's not a scar, but it looks like one. My mother has a huge scar across her stomach, skin wrinkling around it, from having had a cesarean. I was always told that she got her scar when I was born, and I always told her that my scar was a faint shadow of hers, given to me when I was born. But whenever I would say this she would tell me this was untrue—she would pick me up, twirl me around, and sing, in her happiest tone, *Don't worry, baby! Everything will turn out alllllllll right.*

They were first brought to Guam, and then to Fort Indiantown Gap refugee camp. Eventually a church sponsored them and donated a house, winter jackets, and beds. I don't know much more about those first few years. I know that the kids were enrolled in schools, and that on the first day they were taught to say, "My name is [   ], and I live by the church down the road." I know that one day, after phone call after phone call and form after form, Ông arrived at the house. I know from a photo they kept in a glass cabinet that when the first car was bought and brought home they measured the marvelous lengths with their hands. I know from a very early memory that for a while they owned a laundromat, but then one day they did not, and then when the kids became teenagers they went to work in a warehouse that my other grandparents owned. And that's where my parents met.

Bà never learned English, never drove, and even though she was a nurse in Vietnam, she mostly worked as a seamstress and took care of her children and grandchildren. Her big fear was that the motherland would be lost forever, and this was a valid fear—the motherland *would* be lost forever. My mom would complain that she was only allowed to have friends who were Vietnamese, but there were no other Vietnamese people around to be friends with. In high school, she was invited to a pool party and went out and bought herself a bikini, fire engine red like Phoebe Cates's in *Fast Times at Ridgemont High,* and when Bà found it, she cut it all up in disgust. My mom would tell me this story over and over again when I was a child, to imply that she understood and protected my freedom. Since she didn't let me watch *Fast Times,* I had no idea how sexy or sexualized that red bikini scene actually was. Instead, I would imagine this scene of the cut-up bikini like the intro to *The Graduate,* a film she loved, where Benjamin, home from college for the summer, floats across his swimming pool in an existential ennui, to Simon and Garfunkel's song "The Sound of Silence," a song which she also loved, except instead of dapples of light across the water, red nylon scraps of fabric tumble across the bedspread. Snip, snip, snip. It reminds me of her matter-of-fact way of explaining how to manage your social milieu: When something's not working, you cut. Edit. You cut.

My mom's engagement to my dad, the man whose family ran the company at which her brothers worked, who would come over some weekends to play the guitar in their family band that covered Vietnamese folk songs, in which my mom was the lead singer, was basically the worst of all Bà's possible paranoias, far, far worse than a bikini-clad pool party, and my mom was just 18 years old. Bà refused to let her go. Omi came over and knocked on the door. "They are happy!" Omi said. "She's not ready!" Bà said.

My mom saw things differently. "Let me live my life!" she shouted, and left with Omi and a bagful of her most precious things.

Her youngest sister was seven at the time. She tells me that when my mom left, she was sleeping, and suddenly she woke to the darkness pressing down on her. Ran to the side of the room to turn on the light. The darkness vanished, and she fell asleep again.

In the kitchen, Omi picked up the phone. My mom's oldest sister was calling.

"I'm not here," said my mom.

"Why?" asked Omi. Every time she tells me this story, she's sure to explain that if my mom came to the phone, her sister would tell her to come home, and she would have to obey.

My aunt said, "Please put my sister on the phone."

A pause. "She won't come to the phone."

The receiver was given to the next oldest sister. "Please put my sister on the phone."

A pause. "She won't come to the phone."

The receiver was given to the next oldest sister. "Please put my sister on the phone."

A pause. "I'm sorry, but she won't come to the phone."

A pause. The receiver was returned to the oldest sister. "Then please tell her that her sister is gone."

I can imagine this scene, at the beige phone attached to the wall, next to the burnt orange bulletin board tacked with coupons, delivery menus, and phone numbers scrawled in Omi's deliciously loopy handwriting. Omi would probably be leaning against the wall, my mom at the round table, long hair hanging down her back. Or maybe it was at the phone in the living room, Omi on one gray couch, my mom on the other. That version is less interesting, because everything went down in the kitchen. Whereas across her long split-level home we would all disperse into our own days, the kitchen was where we would all clump together.

"Do you remember when you were little how much we wrote together?" Omi asked me once. "We set up a little table for you in the kitchen. You would say a word and I would say a word and we would make a poem.

"We tried to give you a home when your mother left," she continued. "I remember her as a child… a beautiful child."

...One...
...Star...
...To...
...Star...
...In...
...One...
...Wave...
...To...
...Wave!...

"End of poem, Omi!"

I have never gotten a straight story about what happened to her sister, whether it was sickness, suicide, disappearance, disowning, or accidental death, and I have never wanted to ask because I sensed it caused everyone pain. When my mom moved to New York, I would fantasize that we'd be walking down the street one day, and we'd just bump into her sister, like in a movie, sipping on a Diet Coke and looking exactly like my mom, just in a wildly different outfit. "You left a big hole in my life," my mom would sob. "My sister and my best friend."

Her sister might be in a bad place, but my mom would convince her to come home, promise to take care of her. They would hug and cry, and everything would be restored. On the drive to Pennsylvania, I would turn to her and say, "My auntie, why did you leave my mommy when she needed you most?"

"I had been lonely for a very long time," she would say. "When your mommy left, I had no one and I wanted to disappear."

I would turn and look out the window, see my face reflected, with my mother and her sister reflected behind me as the trees passed us by, doing their dance among blue skies and power lines. Just like in the movies, this kind of shot shows a quality of thinking, that the thinker exists in that thin plane of glass where inside and outside gather, shadows falling across her face. Except that if my mom were driving, with her sister next to her in the front seat, there would be no way to catch their reflection behind me as I gazed out the backseat window. Nevertheless, they were always there.

I've never told my mom about this daydream, because she never seemed to want to talk about her. She never, ever mentioned her, except for one day, in 1995, when she took me to a large rock in a field, and cried in front of the rock. Then she told me to cry for her sister. I cried, and crying, grieved for all the mysteries my mother held in her heart and did not tell me, or tell herself.

I honestly don't know how much stock to put into each individual occurrence. My mother was a teenager when I was born, a teenager when she lost her sister, and an adolescent when she left Vietnam. All of these dramatic changes in these delicate developmental years happened too fast for any of us to track in real time. We have to go back to our memories, which are deceitful, or the half-formed observations of any of us who could relate to her. You have to look at her developing relationship to objects, to beauty, to self, and consider what forms of liberation or empowerment exist in that economy for a person like her in her particular circumstance. You could allow yourself to ponder that certain mental illnesses arise in teen years, as all of us have. We will never really know *why* she left everything behind, compulsively, and I'm afraid if I arrive too definitively at any answer, I'll straighten out a crooked story that has always wanted to run warped and wayward. Wild and free.

They were married quickly after. My mom wore her sister's earrings, which she never took off again. She called them her immortal earrings. Nine months later, I was born.

I have seen pictures of the wedding, my mom and my dad surrounded by my German family. When I ask where my mom's family was, Omi tells me that she was told that they didn't want to come. But one day, having inherited a bunch of boxes from my childhood, I found the wedding invitations addressed to her family: sealed, unstamped, unsent. I never asked my mom why she didn't invite them, if she was angry, or for what reason. I learned very quickly, and at a very young age, how futile such questions really were en route to any story that made any sense at all. Different stories would be told, with different explanations, often with contradictions. If I should protest and say that she made me live in a world where I had no truth to believe in, she would say I'm your mother and I brought you into this world, and I'll make the rules of this world. She would also say, I suffered in a way that you will never suffer, and my love for you will protect you from all possible forms of pain. I know that she said all this earnestly, even if I learned not to believe her. I loved her, and unloved her, and then learned to love her for her declarations of love for me, and I learned that she loved me as much as she was capable of loving anyone at all.

By the time I was old enough to remember, everything was back at the beginning: My parents were no longer together, and she saw her family almost every day. She was an unhappy mother, an unhappy wife, and an unhappy daughter. She saw no way out of the life she had made for herself, which was never as good or as effortless or as happy ending-ed as the life she believed she was destined to lead, so she meticulously art-directed everything available to her: her daughter, her home, her voicemail, and the major currency available to her: her beauty. When she would sit at the table with her mother and sisters, my mom would take out her hair to redo it, and it would fall down to the ground and cover the floor, hanging long to her ankles, black. I would run over to touch it, enchanted. Years later, in her absence, she would leave me a pink silk shawl with long black fringe, and in the mornings, I would wake up and pull the knots out of it. I would say that I was combing my mother's hair. I imagined that, like Rapunzel, I could climb down my tower and stand on the Earth, and like Penelope, I would weave and unweave her hair until she came home. I imagined her hair as a river, a rope. I imagined being taken from where I was. And so, I imagined her hair as a myth. But I also imagined her hair as other, darker things. Shadows over my eyes. A disguise. A curtain, whose job it was to fall across the doors and windows of my cage. I imagined that while she set off for calmer waters, I walked the labyrinth of my cage, alone, again and again. This wasn't a cute sentiment, and I was often resentful, bottling up all my resentment under a stony façade. I was a child who appeared emotionless, a grotesque expression of the life she wanted to have, but couldn't have, and everything that she didn't get that she felt she deserved from her life, which she felt had been broken, through bad luck or curse or karma, she impressed onto me: her eternal audience, her dystopic mirror, spinning her out from whatever image she wanted to eat, drink, or inhale of herself in that moment. She always had a way of conjuring in me metaphors of indigestion.

Before my mom traded that particular iteration of herself in for the next one, she loved to sing: Celine Dion and Bette Midler, Vietnamese and American pop songs. At Galaxy Night Club in Fairfax, Virginia, for my uncle's three hundred person wedding, she shuffled and swanned around the ballroom with long, long black hair, bangs hair-sprayed high, áo dài. She and three of her brothers were debuting a song and had practiced for months until they got their harmonies just right. Kind of like The Partridge Family, I thought hopefully. When the time came around for them to perform, we were all so wound up with anticipation that it was as if Mariah Carey were alighting the stage. My mom had not let me wear my glasses for the occasion, and so I padded my way to the stage in an avant-garde dress my mom had picked out for me, to hear them and applaud. "Thank you, thank you," she breathed into the microphone. "Anh," she said, addressing her brother, the groom, and smiling so hard one dimple appeared on her right cheek: "*Just remember in the winter far beneath the bitter snows, lies the SEED that with the sun's love in the spring becomes THE ROSE.*"

Growing up, my mom would take me to Bà's house every day to take care of me while she hung out with her sisters. She seemed happier there, and was always the life of the party, always talking and laughing the loudest. I loved the cacophony of the house. So many siblings, so many cousins, like a giant octopus. It made me feel bigger than myself and blocked out a feeling that would always ball up in the pit of my stomach, a bubblegummy sensation between melancholy and grief that I simply called The Feeling. I have The Feeling now, I would say to my youngest aunt, my favorite, and I would crawl onto her lap and she would rub my back, giving me little pinches up the spine, and as my grandmother, mother, and aunts sat around the kitchen table talking and filling the room with laughter and sound, my uncles' music drifting up from the basement, I would close my eyes and stretch the glorious moment to eternity, gathering its steam like my grandmother's yellow knit tea cozy. I knew that The Feeling came from the knowledge that I could not stay in this space, this moment, this circle forever. Immanently I would be taken from it and my world would go quiet; I would be moved between my parents' homes where the thing that was missing would fill the space with its silent specter. I illuminated this endless space and time with reading, or watching TV, or doing homework, so still and so compliant so as not to unravel anything.

Maybe I liked the octopus-feeling at Bà's house because I couldn't disturb the chaos. There was always a cousin to play with, an aunt to curl my hair, or take me out, or make me a snack, there was always an uncle to build forts with me, then pretend to be the Bogeyman and knock it all down. There was always music in one room, TV in another, cooking in another, everyone making lots of noise. What must that feel like in the world, I would marvel, to have so many other tentacles to guide you? And so the warmth of the kettle, tea, and laughter was luxurious to me, sitting in the middle of this circle. I wanted nothing else, but I wonder if my mother, denied entry into the glamorous, Kodak-colored world of American teenager-dom, wanted something that circle of laughter couldn't provide, or what might be disguised under the sounds of everyone laughing. As I got older, I learned what people meant when they said that laughter is the very best medicine, but as a child, I was just a sponge. Living, absorbing, sensing. Sometimes I miss how much I felt without digesting. I still love yellow kitchens.

During the day, I would sit with Bà while she did the laundry, vacuumed the house, cooked food, prayed at her shrine, and watched soap operas. I would draw portraits of her in the clothes that she wore every day: black pants, a white collared shirt with a square front pocket, and silver house slippers, her hair drawn into a bun. One day she changed into an áo dài and put on her large brown tinted sunglasses and black leather pocketbook, spritzing herself with perfume. I told her that she looked very glamorous. I felt, at the time, that all of the women in my family were like stars, as equally luminous and as far away from the suburban women of Pennsylvania as anyone I saw on TV. Bà responded that her style was French. "One day," she said, "I will teach you how to look French." Then she counted to ten in French. I counted with her.

She took me grocery shopping and to a toy store. We admired a doll with real brown hair and eyelids that closed. It even smelled like baby's breath. We stood staring at the doll for half an hour, then Bà bought it for me and we brought her home and sat her in a little chair. Every day we combed her hair. Because I was always at her house, from dawn till dusk and often overnight, sleeping in between my two youngest aunts, Bà kept half of her drawers full of my clothes, and the doll and I shared a wardrobe. When I would leave her house, to stay with my mother or father or Omi and Opi, I would find comfort in the doll still being there, in place of me, and I believed that as long as it was still there, as long as my grandmother still combed its hair, as long as my aunts still slept beside it, I was somehow *also* still there, the place that I felt I belonged. It did not make The Feeling go away, but it was all I could do: believe that the doll and I were surrogates, that we could live vicariously through one another.

When I was born, Bà's youngest was 9 and her oldest were having babies of their own. My mom was 20, and not really interested in the tedium of baby-raising, so Bà did most of it for her. She didn't really want the baby-raising to end anyway; that's what she would tell me when I would ask why she was always the one taking care of me, when my other cousins were fed, bathed, and clothed by their own mothers. She would tell me that I was her number 13. I would feel very lucky.

The third time my mom left home we were not home at all; we were at the mall. She took me and my aunt, her youngest sister, dress shopping at Limited Too, and agreed that for every dress I wanted to try on, she would get to pick out a dress for me to try on, and she would decide from there.

A commercial was playing when we entered in which middle-school girls walk into a locker like it's a secret passage. The locker grows clouds and becomes a spa. The girls relax luxuriously in their digital blue not-a-cloud-in-the-sky world. The bell rings, they cross through the locker door, and they're in the world again. Limited Too was my mom's favorite place to shop for me, but I found it too colorful, too trendy, too garish. My style, at the time, was anything that made me disappear, which meant outfits exactly like every average middle-class girl in suburban Pennsylvania. A spaghetti strap tank top, for example, with a pair of khaki capris. Hers was what she called "classy": white linens with wide legs and matching blazers, stilettos, and red lipstick, her long hair in a loose braid. Every month we drove for hours to the outlet mall where she meticulously perused the racks of Off Saks and I read in the carts or hid under the hanging garments. We would march up and down the long halls hunting for deals, or she would reward me with two books from B. Dalton and a stack of tabloids for herself, parking us at the pay phones to chat with friends and admirers for hours, dumping quarter after quarter into the slot, laughing as I worked my way through the entire *Sweet Valley High* series. For some reason, in kids clothes, her preferred style for me always included shirts with dayglo flowers made out of plastic, or tiny skorts in neon plaid with knee socks and oxfords, clothes that implied precocious American confidence and exuberance, even though I could muster none of those things. Holding my *Sweet Valley High* books only semi-open so as not to crack their spines, I longed for Jessica and

Elizabeth Wakefield's SoCal-spun golden hair, cerulean blue eyes, and tan skin, as ardently as I desired the long, straight dark hair of my mother, my grandmother, my aunts, and my cousins, as all of the women I was related to, except for Omi, who herself possessed the coveted blonde curls and cornflower blue eyes. I gazed longingly at my mother through descriptions of *The Baby-Sitters Club*'s Claudia Kishi, who had long, silky black hair. In *Sweet Valley High*, I admired how even though Jessica was fun-loving and popular and Elizabeth was thoughtful and bookish, their personalities still found normative forms of social success like being on the cheerleading squad and editor-in-chief of the school newspaper. Most importantly, I admired how they somehow found a way to be the best of friends.

The first dress I tried was my mom's choice. It made me feel like an ugly doll pretending to be a pretty doll. "I love it," she announced.

"I hate it!" I could already feel tears stinging my eyes. "It's just not me!"

"What do you mean it's not *YOU*?!" my mom yelled in the fitting room, which was unnecessary since it wasn't bigger than a fridge.

In a hushed voice, to cancel out her screaming, I whispered: "It's just not my personality."

"How do you know that? *I* think it's your personality!" my mom exclaimed. "And I should know—I'm your mother after all!"

"It's just my opinion," I shrugged. I suggested a white dress with puffy sleeves trimmed with lace.

"Blegh!" she pretended to vomit. She asked me where I'd learned this word *opinion*. She said I was too young to even understand what that meant, but that I was old enough to disrespect her, and too young to know exactly how lucky I was, because she had given me everything, and I had no idea what it was like to have nothing, like she did when she was my age. Her voice rose with each sentence.

My aunt, in a quiet voice, asked what would be the harm if she let me wear what I liked.

"This isn't about that!" my mom shrieked. "I've sacrificed and sacrificed to give her everything I never had. MY LUCK that I got the bad seed. Do you know what our mother said to me when I was pregnant with her? She said that karma would give me a bad daughter, because I had been a bad daughter. And do you know what? *She was right.*"

I wanted to fall dramatically to the ground and bury my face in my hands like I had seen lots of little girls do on TV when they wanted to have a good cry, but she gripped me hard by the arm. I kept going limp and she kept yanking me up. I wanted to disappear, in a very different way than I did when I wore spaghetti straps and khakis. I imagined the camera panning through the door of the dressing room to happy mothers and daughters shopping quietly in the still, motionless, heavily air-conditioned air, so close to me but still untouchable, and behind them, Limited Too's four walls, covered in huge, neon daisies and pictures of beautiful, smiling, well-dressed girls. I became so small that I almost dissolved, while they grew larger in my mind, larger and larger until they began to take on volume, filling up all the air in the room, sucking up all the oxygen, pushing on me and making me miniscule while girls and daisies danced, waving their arms in the air and slowly morphing into monsters, glamorous monsters, classy monsters, confident and exuberant with red lipstick and long, silky braids dragging across the floor.

Too bad, I can only remember these scenes like shots in a film, the story of her leaving me. "Wait right here," she said to me and my aunt, her youngest sister, just a teenager, the one I followed everywhere and was always next to, in the breezeway of the mall, that little area between entrances that blasts you with heat when crossing from outside to inside. "I'll be right back with the car." Standing against the glass doorway, we played a game of Twenty Questions while we watched the darkness swallow my mother until we could not see her. We passed hours with our faces against the glass, waiting, but she didn't come back for us. After a while, my aunt understood that she was the protector. Tightening her grip on my hand, she opened the door to search for my mother. Crossed the parking lot for what felt like miles, as though it was a treadmill, rolling endlessly on like a song skipping or on repeat.

Looking for the house, guided by some internal compass, the girls cross bridges, meadows, and forests. *I'm scared!* says one. *We're lost in another world!* says another. At the edge of the woods, they find the Farmer Selling Watermelons, standing like a sentinel outside of the house. Like Gorgeous's father and Mr. Togo, the only other male characters in the film, he never enters the house. Instead, he points the house out to the girls, on top of a hill, saying, "We haven't had visitors for a looooong time." His watermelon is spray-painted black, with a vine sprouting out of it, like a bomb. He taps happily on the watermelon. It sounds like a bomb, too, but the girls do not hear this and continue on.

My aunt and I walked towards a mist, carried by the wind, arrived at an empty pool lined with immortal earrings. At the bottom of the pool was an ice skating rink with lots of little girls twirling around on the ice. We shimmied down the sides. She showed me how to shimmy. At the bottom of the pool, we danced around in our sneakers, using the ice to slide. Scintillating light glinted across the ice. I was both dazzled and overwhelmed.

In the movie in my mind, we claw our way out of the gemstone pool and my dad pulls up to us as though he's been just around the corner waiting. We pile into the car and say nothing. We feel immaculate relief. We allow ourselves to be moved and brought home. Sometimes in the car we'd be so comfortable we'd allow ourselves to be rocked to sleep.

As the years have passed, I've grown skeptical of this memory of a pool lined with gemstones, with an ice skating rink at the bottom. When I asked my aunt about it, she said that it just wasn't true. There's no such thing as a mall with a gemstone pool, much less in Pennsylvania. She insisted that we'd never left the breezeway. That yes, my dad had come to pick us up. But no, it hadn't been that long. The rest of it I had totally imagined.

The death we forget about in *House* is, of course, the mother's. After this scene, Gorgeous does not really attend to it. Of course, if you want to write a story about a-young-girl-who-dreams-of-snipping-her-tethers, the easiest way to get at the gut is to remove the mother, make her evil or alienate the bond. Every creator of a Disney princess has followed this practice. I should know—I was paying attention to motherless girls throughout my childhood. Jotting notes: How big is the shape she left behind? How deep was the empty pool? It took a long time to answer these questions because I was absolutely intimate with the estrangement. But by putting these notes together, cutting, editing, collaging, organizing, and reorganizing, I began to understand the story of what happened. My mother, receiving a new life on a boat, mirrored this estrangement in the portrait of her relationship with herself, becoming very much like: a boat. And though I immediately understood that she had left, it was a long time before I understood that she was only coming back as a ghost.

Lots of things changed after that. I would see my mom every other weekend and for one month in the summer, and I saw Bà even less, and as the years went on, when I did have the opportunity to see Bà, I wasn't comfortable without my mom there, my chain link in the family constellation. My grasp of Vietnamese froze, even declined, and it was harder and harder for Bà and I to get to know one another as we grew older, and I didn't have the words to say that to her, so I don't know if she ever understood. Sometimes she would call me to tell me that she had changed my doll's clothes or brushed her hair, and as The Feeling would fill my gut I would respond, ask her if she had looped the hair into many buns like the Spice Girls or a low bun that matched hers. These conversations never seemed infantile to me no matter how old the two of us got—it was just something to talk about, in a realm of language we both shared. We were always expressing something else: something swimming under the surface.

My mom cut her hair into a shaggy bob and moved hours away, to New York City. Some weekends she would pick me up and we would driiiiiiive for what felt like forever, not on the open road, but in traffic, my mom cranking the volume, singing alongside her favorite singers, the golden voices of Gloria Gaynor and Karen Carpenter. Exiting the Holland Tunnel, I would start singing, to the tune of Shirley Bassey's "Kiss Me, Honey, Honey, Kiss Me," circle, circle, circle, circle, over and over again, louder and louder, joyously coming into view of city streets folded into one another until we were both shouting, *CIRCLE, CIRCLE, CIRCLE, CIRCLE! CIRCLE, CIRCLE, CIRCLE, CIRCLE!* When I think about those weekends and summers, in places where I had no friends or anything to do, I remember us passing time with no agenda at all but to "be together," and this always felt unnatural. Not that we shouldn't be together, but that I shouldn't have anything else, anything else in the world to do but spend my time with her, in a blank void that hurled itself suddenly gobsmack into my normal, everyday life.

When I was older, she would tell me that she had left our family to reclaim a freedom lost, to grow up, and I understand, and I don't know anything other than what it is for her to be gone, staying with her from time to time, a mother more like a sister, more like a balloon, angled towards the sky and pushing against its tethers, against gravity, and even though I understand, I don't think it's fair: Her desire for her freedom was my little prison—it kept me in her cage.

Outside the house, Fantasy leans in to take a picture. "Say cheese!" she says.

"Butter!"

"Margarine!"

"Jam!"

"Sexy!"

As the cat Blanche makes eye contact with the camera, it falls and breaks. Fantasy is spooked. Now nothing she sees will exist. Mac presents to Auntie their gift: a watermelon.

Auntie's house is painted in shades of gray. It's covered in dust. Not even the fridge works. Still, there are signs of life: "Dear Chandelier," says Auntie, "Shine on them!" The chandelier *turns on*. The house *turns on*. Auntie admits to being lonely.

"But now I have many young girls in my house," she says to her coven—seven smiling girls. Teenagers, each with their own individual style, laugh line, and set of props: Gorgeous, all in white. Prof, in her glasses. Kung Fu, in an army-green two piece, who will kick off her clothes and spend the rest of the film in a bikini bottom and tank top. Mac, in a checkered jumpsuit, snacking the whole time. Melody, with her violin. Fantasy, all in pink. Wandering the forest hand in hand to Godiego's soundtrack song:

I see in your eyes
Where tomorrow
Is hiding
In my heart

What does that all mean anyway? That the image holds the future in its face? That it's this desire towards which they are running? It's sort of like a sunrise, emerging out of the horizon, moving from the melancholy of dawn to morning's activity, refracting light like a shining chandelier.

"Teenagers," Omi would always interrupt, when I was a teenager and would lie out by the pool, sun browning my skin. "I was never a *'teenager.'*"

The girls set to work cleaning the dust from the house, opening the windows to light. Prof decides that she's in charge until their teacher, Mr. Togo, comes to join them. Color enters the rooms. The house "wakes up." Becomes animated. Soon everything is alive. Auntie calls to the stove.

"I talk with the furniture as I work," Auntie says.

Mac, holding the watermelon, turns to the fridge. "Dear fridge—may I cool this in you?"

"It's out of order!" Auntie declares proudly. "How about a natural refrigerator?"

"You mean a well? How wonderful!"

Mac, Gorgeous, and Auntie journey to the well. Dropping the bulbous, bomb-sounding watermelon into the well, the well hears them wonder, from within its pool of water, "What if we lose it?"

Bà's house is the house of my dreams. Anytime I dream of a house, it's hers: I open the front door to her living room, and there's her kitchen in front of me and a stairway to the left. It's my elemental house, the stage for my psyche. In some dreams there is a chandelier, even though there was no chandelier in her house. Sometimes the chandelier hangs from the ceiling. Sometimes it lays on the floor. In every dream, Bà sits at the base of the stairs and is crying, crying, as all of her children kneel around her and cry too, as she and they did the day a drunk man crashed into my uncle's car, and she began to sob, screaming and crying, and I stood scared by the door, not understanding what had happened, except that my beloved grandmother, queen of this house and my world, was in an out-of-control kind of pain, and I was too afraid to go to her. In the dream I am still watching, still far away, still small, still unable to ask or to understand. My Bà, why are you crying?

But Omi's house is the house I know in my heart. I know the sound of every door: if it slides, if it's spring loaded, if it has wind chimes hung from its knob. It is my earliest instrument, where each sound is a sonic coordinate to my emotional life. I know the creak of every stair, the pressure of the water in every faucet, the temperature of every lamp, the rustle of each individual branch on each window. I know the smell of every room, its atmosphere, its mood according to the time of day, the threads of the carpets under my feet, their texture.

I was an insomniac when I was a child, and terrified of the dark. Omi was an insomniac, too—this was our shared curse—and wore bells around her ankles, and so as long as I could hear the sound of her walking around in the kitchen, of the bells on the carpet, in the living room, I would feel safe, her moving by foot, by neck, sometimes singing to her mother, whom she called Mami, and of whom I have one memory, standing in the doorway leaning on her cane. Omi always said that Mami was nervous and an exaggerator, and that I inherited this from her. That I am melodramatic, and that I inherited this from her, Omi. And that all three of us are famous for hating onions.

If I was still awake and she had gone to bed, and I had heard her turning off the lights, and there were no more sounds whatsoever, no more bells, that's when I would plunge into fear, imagining kidnappers and other criminals I saw when Opi watched *Matlock* or *Columbo*, coming to take me away. I memorized the figures in shapes in the peeling wallpaper, and I understood their personalities by the stoops of their shoulders. They emerged from the walls and the secret passages I imagined behind heavy curtains, like in *The Secret Garden*, filling the empty air around me. Intoxicated by *The Secret Garden*, having read the book and watched the 1993 film adaptation, I imagined I was Mary Lennox, a sickly, surly, motherless girl with tangled hair in an old, giant house, exploring abandoned chamber after abandoned chamber, until one day, in yet another abandoned chamber, I would hear the sound of someone crying. "There's someone crying!" I'd insist with desperation. "There's someone crying!" One night, I would follow the sound of the crying until I found another person my age squirreled away in the house. Secretly we would strike a friendship, plant a garden, build strength in parts of our spirits that had gone uncultivated. Sometimes, swinging alone on my grandparents' swing set, the momentum of my swinging would move the swing next to me, so it was easy to imagine another person there. A kind of twin. A present absence. I was inspired by the metaphor of the walled garden, and that Mary Lennox was always breaking down doors.

In Bà's house, I was never Mary Lennox: The vibe didn't fit. Instead, my cousins and I were obsessed with technology and video games. We would role-play Sonic the Hedgehog or Street Fighter, running around the house and shouting, "Hadouken! Hadouken!" shooting our wrists forward to release fireballs. Sometimes we would play dead and try to scare people, leaning up suddenly to shout, "Hadouken!" One time, my cousin scared me so much a whole glass of orange juice shot out of my nose. We would make up our own X-Men, and once I swear I invented the internet. "I have a computer," I shouted to my cousins, jabbing my pointer finger around in the air, "which will tell me ANYTHING I WANT TO KNOW!" They told me I was a huge dork.

My aunts would always tell me that Bà would worry that I would forget that I was Vietnamese, that she would tell my mom that she should be stricter, that she shouldn't speak English with me, that she shouldn't take me shopping so much because if I became dazzled by money and things I would believe that to be American was to be rich, to be German was to be rich, but to be Vietnamese was to be poor, and I might choose to disinherit myself. "She won't forget," my mom would always say, rolling her eyes. "She's very down to earth. Do you know what she wants to be? A *writer*."

But my grandmother took it upon herself to map me into the world. "When you tell people you're Vietnamese," she instructed me, "tell them your grandmother is from Haiphong."

She made me practice saying this phrase several times in Vietnamese: "My grandmother is from Haiphong."

"I thought we came from Saigon," I objected.

"First we lived in Haiphong, in the north."

"Why did we move to Saigon?"

"We had to."

"Is it far?"

"Very far."

"What's it look like?"

"It's very beautiful, and there's lots of water. Lots and lots of water."

On summer days an aunt or uncle would take us in a gaggle across the backyard, through a thin row of trees, to the community pool. In the water, with our eyes closed, they would shout, "One, two, three!" throwing a whole pile of coins into the air. We would dive down into the biggest bowl of blue

Jell-O there ever was, heading first for the big silver coins, the quarters, and pick up as many as we could in one breath, emerging with fistfuls of money and shouting, "I'm rich! I'm rich! I'm rich!" I practiced a lot, each time imagining I was a mermaid, that my swimming was a kind of dancing. Sometimes my mom came to the pool too, but didn't swim very well, so she'd hold on to the concrete ledge and kick-kick-kick her back legs in the water. Bà never, ever went with us to the pool.

Omi, on the other hand, loved to swim. On sunny days we would take the pool floats out of the garage and throw them onto the sparkling water. We would make pink lemonade, scooping powdery Country Time sugar crystals into glasses printed with psychedelic patterns, or make bowlfuls of Breyer's Vanilla Fudge Twirl ice cream topped with raspberry syrup, eating at a table underneath an umbrella. Then we would race across the pool or cannonball off of the diving board or I would lay on a float and she would mimic a gently rolling wave. I loved her burnt orange and brown towels and striped lawn chair cushions and the feeling of wet hair and sun on my shoulders. I loved to put on my goggles and flip around underwater to look at the sky, breathing bubbles through my nostrils for as long as it took the clouds to move.

I always understood that both of my grandmothers would be the great mother-losses of my life, but I chose not to think about it. I did not know how to think about it; when I did The Feeling would swell inside me, thick and gummy and pressing against my pores. But one day, many years after my mom had left, when my childhood was fully over, I got a call that Bà had suffered a deadly stroke, and I realized that I had not prepared myself for this death that had so many layers. She had been placed on life support and an unplugging was scheduled for the coming Saturday so that everyone had time to come and say goodbye. I drove home. In the hospital, the family filled the room. It was the first time we had all been together in many years, and the last, for many years after. Arriving on the arm of an aunt, Ông started talking to Bà in her coma. He said that they had had a dozen children together, that they had spent forty years raising children looking forward to the days when it would be just the two of them again, that soon after the last moved out she had gotten sick, but that in the few months of their freedom it had been like when they'd first met: Haiphong, 1953, a young nurse and a young public servant, holding hands on the boulevards, and that he feels robbed of the opportunity to devote the rest of his life to loving her, that his only hope for the future would be to find her in the afterlife and never be apart again.

That was the most I'd ever heard him say, then or since. For most of my childhood, he went to work and came home, sat in a chair, watched TV, and smoked cigarettes, handing me a box of orange Tic-Tacs whenever I approached him. I didn't understand anything he said to my grandmother. Sitting next to my aunt, she whispered the translation in my ear.

One by one we approached my grandmother's body. When it was my turn, I held her hand, dry and bluish. I had not spoken Vietnamese in years. I did not have many words to use to talk to her, and I had an audience. I told her that I loved her, and I missed her, and that I was sorry, so sorry to have not gone to see her while she was sick but still alive and there to talk to. I touched my forehead to her forehead for the very last time. I touched the cold stone of her jade bracelet. Secretly, I imagined a space for us to inhabit together, manically cycling through every memory I had: she, watching Chinese soap operas and folding baskets of clothes, Downy detergent filling my nose. She, holding me on her lap and squeezing all of my preteen curves. She, taking a mango from her shrine to cut it up into a flower. *We two who eat fruit*, is how I understood the translation of what she would say to me in Vietnamese. We two eating it.

The day before they pulled the plug, my mom had still not arrived from New York. I texted her: *Where are you?* There was no response for a few hours. Then, calling me by the word for daughter, she wrote:

Con! Can't get a day off of work
Been asking for DAYS
Then flights are booked
Can't get in til Sun
Do you think it's gonna be okay?

I felt responsible for two people: my mother and my grandmother. I thought that my mother trusted that I wouldn't be cruel, and this would protect her from the truth. I wanted to be honest without being cruel, so I wrote, in the most indirect syntax I could use to express the truth directly,

She will be dead by Sunday.

After they pulled the plug, it took her a day to die. My aunts worried that it was because she had always told them proudly that all of her ancestors had waited for all of their children to gather to say goodbye, and my mother still hadn't arrived. But she didn't wait. We were in the kitchen, everyone laughing, and the news that she had died came through the doorway, spreading from left to right as we turned to stone.

The next day my mother arrived, bursting into my aunt's house sobbing, clutching me, digging her hands into my arm, telling me how much she had suffered, how hard she had to work to provide for me, so hard that they didn't even let her go to see her own mother die, which I didn't understand, because I was an adult, living on my own and working, paying my own rent and everything, and besides that, she hadn't raised me, had hardly made a dent in the money pit it took to raise a child. It's not that I wasn't grateful for the things that she'd done, it's that I deeply resented being roped into the reason why she had missed her mother's death, and I deeply resented the belief that all these years, she insisted that her story was one of sacrificial single-motherness, while I felt that I'd barely had a mother at all. Growing up, most nights, I had eaten dinner without her, and every evening I diligently did my homework and my father diligently checked it and explained all of my mistakes. On weekends he took me to ham fests and car rallies or we played chess or ping-pong or did our own thing in separate corners of the house. At night I would shower and sit in a little red chair while he combed and blow-dried my hair. Every morning he got up, made me breakfast, and I took the 6 a.m. bus to school, which he also set up to drop me off at a nearby after-school program. I got dressed alone, and got my period alone. In public, from a very young age, I went to the women's bathrooms alone while he waited outside. When I reached puberty, I, on my own, found a local boarding school, and, on my own, applied for a scholarship, got that scholarship, and my father and I agreed that it would probably be best for me to go. I lived from then on surrounded by women. The idea that she could rescue me by taking me out and about every other weekend seemed to negate the tedium, humiliation, and small joys of raising a human being every single day, the mothering that everyone, including me, did in her absence. Nor did it ever acknowledge my quietly accumulating rage.

"Stay!" she said. "I need you!" I stayed one more night. My mom, the fun one, the beautiful one, the prodigal one, went hunting for tequila and got everyone drunk. Except this time, it felt different. She laughed a little too loud, made jokes that seemed outdated. I hadn't heard her speak Vietnamese in so long; it seemed like another person that she all of a sudden slipped into, using the familiar voice she once used when sitting around the kitchen table, when gossiping with the women who cut my hair at Hair Cuttery, or the four sisters who owned the phở restaurant that we loved to eat at, peppering her sentences with "you" because there is no direct translation for the way that word is used in English. She was playing the person I once recognized as my mom, which made me wonder if she was ever that person at all. Maybe I had grown up knowing someone who was just a façade. Or maybe she had just grown up, become someone in whom being a mom, or a daughter, or a sister did not take up much space. Whatever, or whoever, she was, she didn't seem to want to be there, and was relying on fun as a smokescreen to perform a familial intimacy that she didn't feel anymore and didn't want to talk about, and she never came home again.

For six hours after her death, Bà's body was left alone, a plastic box of Buddhist chants tucked close to her ear.

Once her spirit had departed, her body remained like a piece of wood. Her face was covered with a white cloth.

At the funeral, monks played gongs and bells and began to sing.

I was moved to tears.

We plucked rose heads from the wreaths surrounding her casket and left them covering her body, cheeks, and hair as we said our final goodbyes.

It's Fantasy who discovers Mac's head in the well, thinking it's the watermelon cooling.

As she pulls the watermelon up by the rope, she is distracted by the beautiful sunset.

"How beautiful!" she says, admiring the sky, holding Mac's head in her hands.

She looks down.

At a shrine, my aunts kneeled before her portrait and poured tea into tiny cups and held incense between their hands.

My uncle carried a photograph and incense from the viewing room to the oven and we followed in a line, wearing white headbands while chanting, kneeling in prayer on the cold, hard ground, touching our foreheads to the Earth.

Monks read the names of her descendants in a song, a long drone, tripping at my name.

Fantasy giggles.

Mac calls to her: "*Fantasy!*" Laughing and laughing and laughing.

Fantasy screams, and runs away.

At the cremation, my mom was front and center of the sobbing sisters, clutching me while the box holding her mother's body was hoisted up into the oven, to be cremated and held in a temple where monks would pray for her soul's peaceful passage under the glow of fresh flowers, fruit, and an orange light.

At the temple, monks served us lunch and carried on singing, holding the microphone so close to the mouth we could hear every breath, every pop of lips or bump of shoulder, the microphone bouncing every extra bit of life off the monks' bodies into our bodies, filling us with more sound, more singing.

"A human head!" Fantasy gasps, back in the house.

"Yes—everyone has one," the rest of the girls agree, kindly.

Only Gorgeous comforts her freaked-out friend.

Around the waking house, things absorb Auntie's endless hunger, which is only expanding in euphoria. Though she greeted the girls in a wheelchair and curiously began walking, now she dances in the kitchen while the girls clean up around her. She tells them that she hasn't been this excited since she was a little girl going to a restaurant in town. She plans to savor the girls one by one but eat them while they're still fresh, like oysters.

"Don't worry, Fantasy," she says to the worried girl. "You'll see Mac!" She disappears into the fridge. Fantasy drops her plate in fright.

Prof opens the fridge as if to prove something. "Nothing in here—!"

They don't notice that when they pour water into a glass, it turns to blood. The domestic sounds of dishes, clocks chiming, insects droning, and teacups clinking create a constant musical accompaniment, luring them into poly-temporal states where the mind acts like a sieve, leaving certain memories undigested and dormant until the cell signals to *turn on*. Fearlessly, Gorgeous takes a bath, Melody plays music, Kung Fu breaks open locked doors, and Sweet cleans the house from top to bottom. In a bedroom, she finds a doll. The doll calls to her:

Sweetest Sweet!
I'm a little babydoll
Cutest little babydoll :)

I wanted to leave something in her casket that would help her remember that we all lived together, that she would not be alone, so I made a doll that looked like me, and I chose to use a 4 x 4 beam of wood, which was a fairly standard construction material: thin, but fleshy enough to provide comfort. The beam was composed of Douglas Fir, more textural and corporal than other options at Home Depot, and I had the beam cut down to my size: five foot eight. Looking at the beam laying down on the saw, I felt much smaller than I had previously. I sanded the wood down on all sides. Then I made a small incision into the wood about 1/3 of the way to the top, at the sacral joint. The incision represented my injury, which made my body more disembodied than ever. Then I drilled a hole into the "hip joint" and inserted a vitamin, in hopes that my wounds would heal. Finally, I painted the wood a color called "Lavender Sand," and drew a silver line down the middle. I drew it to the deepest point that I could bend.

The line was a meditation, and a performance of the attempt to honor my multiple selves: the language of my mother, and the language of my father. It was a silver lining, and a meditation to see what shapes emerged, what symmetries. The first symmetry, the symmetry of faces, is the deepest archive, the first reflection, and the longest-lasting. How we understand ourselves as alone comes from those who have left us, a dream past and a dream present whose walls we never live in, but which we are re-creating, again and again, in a dream future far, far away. And the doll became an avatar, emoting for me, soaking up all my sentience—my faces, organs, spores, and bacteria—until I became the doll. Then I cut a hole into the throat and I placed the throat into the casket next to her, because I knew that even though I would be staying here on earth, the language she had given me would be leaving with her.

Sweet reaches for the doll, and the doll reaches back, digs her tiny plastic fingernails into Sweet's fleshy arm. Mirrors, pillows, blankets, and feathers fall on them, alone in the room and with abandon. She screams an operatic sounding scream, and strangest of all, the camera, the thing watching from underneath the glass floor, twirls in delight.

Only Fantasy hears Sweet screaming. She tries to enter the room to save Sweet, but she's locked out. She stares through the door, the door of distortion.

Auntie dances with her cat Blanche, the cat of death, the cat that saw the bomb in the camera. She crawls and waltzes on the ceiling beams, smiling into the camera, as though Auntie, the house, the beams, the cat, and the camera are all complicit in the haunting. And the beams want to be more than just beams, want to be more than just a standard home construction material—they want to build a boat, a story crafted by collision, accident, destruction, and rebuilding, rather than plot. Auntie dreams of all the good things that have finally come home to her, to jaunty music, just before joyously eating a young girl's hand.

For the first 49 days after the funeral, my family held a memorial service every seven days. Incense was burned on the altar every day, and food was presented before each meal to show my grandmother that she was still a part of family life. My family was instructed not to eat meat for sixty days. This only lasted three. After forty-nine days, they stopped bringing rice to the altar. After one hundred days, they celebrated the end of tears, when her transition to residing among the dead ancestors was complete and the new social order—whatever that was—took form. After one year was the ceremony of the anniversary of her death. After three years was the ceremony of the end of mourning. The clothes the family wore to the funeral, and every other memorial service, were burned.

I did not go to any of the memorial services until the ceremony of the end of mourning. In a pot in the yard of a Buddhist temple in Northern Virginia, we burned our white scarves, crippling the air with plasticky fumes. I hadn't seen my cousins since the funeral. They'd had weddings and babies. The next generation! We toasted and cheered. I knew, as the one who was half-white, that it was always thought that I was cold and quiet, and I couldn't shake the feeling that Bà had worried that one day I would forget that I was Vietnamese. I decided that she wasn't wrong to worry. But if I could talk to Bà today, I would want to comfort her, I would tell her that I had never had to endure what she endured, that she had given me the good life, and I would sing, dance, crack her up, buy her clothes, take her swimming, she who once fought so hard against the water, if only she could see me *just float...* Bà! Bà! Bà! I would call to her. Look at me! All around me is the sea!

The last time I saw my grandmother was the last time I saw my mother. When I put on my white headband and touched my forehead to the Earth, I said goodbye to both of them. I didn't mean to test her, but Bà's death was a test. If she couldn't make it home in time for her mother's death, she didn't feel that she owed us anything. She had failed our trust fall.

In the years since, I have written a lot about Bà's death, and I have erased a lot of the writing, unsure why I've been compelled to write about it, particularly since I remember so little, and what stands out in my memory seems to miss the point: what I thought about what she was wearing, her makeup in her casket, her hair cut short at the hospital. In writing, I developed an image in my mind that I returned to again and again, where we were two prisoners in cells next to each other, tapping messages onto the walls with spoons. We developed a code, an alternate alphabet, a way of understanding one another. I was wrong to think that our code wasn't a kind of language, and to think that all those years, as I was let loose out in the world, that she also wasn't moving and changing. I was wrong to believe that I would always find her at home, and home with her, that both would exist always, always returnable, that her death wouldn't also come with its own bureaucracies, that without its matriarch, her home and her family wouldn't also break apart into many pieces without the strength of her hold. I realized that all these years, I relied on my image of her as unchanging in order to believe in something stable, in order to fix the shifting sands beneath me.

She would tell her children that she was not afraid of death. Every day after chanting she would meditate on dying and so death folded itself into the fabric of her life. I imagine that when it finally happened, while her family was together laughing in the kitchen, it was not unlike any other day when she kneeled at the shrine outside her kitchen, it was like opening a door to a room she was quite accustomed to. I imagine that she held it open much longer than we thought she was capable of, to wait for my mother, and so I worried that her journey would be lonely—she who insisted her family travel together, else they be forced apart.

After my accident, I saw general doctors, chiropractors, pain specialists, and physical therapists, and pain management became as habitual as brushing my teeth. The years-long process of "getting better," I discovered, was about learning new habits and accepting that my body, my first home, would never be the same—I could never live in it without fighting against it in some way. In this sense, the body is also a metaphor for home. After all, what is the body but a container, a receptacle of our lives? Even the skin is designed to keep the skeleton from falling apart, to protect it, navigating its organism through its ambient environment, betraying certain information about its internal workings, carrying its own memory of conditions experienced in the remote and immediate past. I thought that if I possessed any great hunger, it was to cohere inside of something like a skeleton inside the skin, the mother of the senses, so comfortably I wouldn't even feel it there, I could disappear inside it and become lost. And now, now that her body was inanimate and untouchable, so was home, and my hunger began growing and growing, more urgent and more desirous than ever before—so insane and insatiable that I moved according to its opposite, I withdrew and I moved away, I was always away, which became another form of containment.

A haunted house is a haunted mind. A ghost floats an expression across her face, haunts the house, the mind, magic, and the mirror, the white cat next to the candle, the pendulum swinging from one generation to the one to come, and in each mirror is a different image. This is why it can be so hard to trust the things you're seeing, and if your mother is a mystery, why should you trust anything? That's when I play a game of imagine. I like to step inside her skin. I like to perform the monologue inside her mind, as a way of stepping outside myself. Like when she's walking around Soho, the neighborhood that she lived in for ten years, on three different corners of the same intersection, and looking at all of these *things* through the windows. A window is a clear wall, and implies that you can't reach beyond the surface. It might be calming, to freeze noise into landscape, to put a glass wall between yourself and the unknowns that threaten you, the unknowns you translate into unreasonable states of fear, to frame a situation like an image—this one, walking endlessly along windows, is it: thinking about things she could maybe have, or have not, or once could not have and now could have. Or not thinking at all. Not thinking at all about what's been lost.

To have and to have not. To want. What does she see in the disfiguring window? Maybe a vision of endurance, and what we can say about it. What we can continue to call the self when we have lost the things we usually say about it. A way to reinhabit the world. A way to act. What do you do when your face is a constant memory?

You dispossess.

You put on a new face.

Here lies Gorgeous, soaking in the bathtub. Suddenly, long black locks rise up from the water to grab her, leading her like a river to her bedroom. The door opens automatically. The light is already on, and there are paper flower sculptures lining the walls. She sits at the dressing stand facing three mirrors, flanked on one side by a bridal gown, on another by a drawing of a white cat. Gazing at herself in the mirrors, she sees her mother, sees Auntie, sees a version of herself reflected. She puts on the lipstick she finds in the drawers.

Auntie [from near and far] I've been lonely.

Like this, she continued to return to me as a ghost. This time, I held her captive as a monster in the mirror, where I visited her on my terms. I conjured whole scenes and stories of the two of us together, a movie in my mind. Sometimes the scenes could be nightmarish, but sometimes they were sweet, and I would replay them again and again, floating inside them like a bug trapped in honey. Sometimes, I would find a way to reconcile myself with the knowledge that she loved me as much as she could, and that was enough, and I could love her back without the burden of defacing myself completely. Or I'd imagine that she'd leave and leave and leave and leave and suddenly, I would turn the key to the door in my mind at a certain angle to find a way for her to stay. To communicate to her what she'd done wrong. To find a way for her to change, to reflect, to feel remorse, and to want me as her daughter. To tell me that she was sorry. To believe her.

Response: The mirror breaks again and again. It cries real tears, rose red. Gorgeous's face and body crack open in flames. Obayashi said that he shot this scene in a mirror, so that he could key out a shard and fill it in with fire. As a result, the special effects are pretty campy, so even though you're bombarded with signs of terror, you know there's nothing to be afraid of. The soundtrack plays a minor chord, so you know you're supposed to feel sad.

THE MATERNAL ECOLOGY

A note

In ancient Greece, theater audiences watched from hillsides, in *theatrons*, or "seeing places," in open air structures consisting of an *orchestra*, in the middle of which was an altar, and behind that, the *skene*. The *skene*, or "tent" or "hut," was used as a backstage area for actors to change masks or costume, doubling also as the play's fictitious location, generally a palace or house. These *skenes*, if permanent, were often painted to serve as backdrops—*scenery*, *facades*, or *screens*—with multiple doors for the entrances of ghosts or gods. Today, in a typical theater space, much of the work of the skene is done by curtains, which may mask, fly, tease, torment, or frame spaces large and small.

The word *fantastic*, in common parlance, means "extraordinarily good or attractive," or "imaginative or fanciful; remote from reality," or "seeming more appropriate to the imagination than to reality." It takes its origin from the Greek *phantastikos*, which takes its origin from *phantazein*, or "make visible"; *phantazesthai*, "have visions, imagine" or "picture to oneself"; and *phantos*, simply "visible."

Ever since I was a little girl, I have lived in a fantastic theatron: a seeing place whose walls keep disappearing, transforming to mask, fly, tease, or torment, and beyond the walls are nothingness, and three generations of women live with me, entering through the door to rehearse their magical future, every character brought down by their character, by the desire to look good as themselves for themselves, and I alone see them, I alone beholding my house, my body, my ghosts and my gods, and my screen that is suddenly a cannibal.

Characters
Karma: *Mother Flower*
Khaos: *Daughter Flower, pregnant*
Sisters: *Also Daughters and Flowers*
Mother
Daughter
Grandmother V
Grandmother Z

Setting
Each domestic space is made of many layers: mother, culture, inherited narrative, law. Dear Reader, know that in every scene we may be in any and all of these layers at once.

Act 1

Scene 1

Setting: the center of a large house, which spans three miles and contains no exit. The house has bright lights, a white kitchen, a beautiful spiral staircase, and no doors to the outside. Cameras and screens are installed onto every surface. On one screen, the film *House* plays, and the mirror breaks again and again, breaks Auntie's face reflected in it and cries real tears, rose red. Watching it all in horror, Gorgeous's face and body crack open to reveal flames. The mirror, too, is in flames. Obayashi made that fire, cutting out the shape of the shards, mirror, and Gorgeous's silhouette, so that the fire stays holding the shape that they are in, as Gorgeous beholds something she has never known: the fracture.

"You'll feel no more pain!" sings Prof as she wraps a Band-Aid around Melody's piano-bitten finger.

On another screen, a heroine lives as if in a disorienting dream, and this represents her overwhelming feeling of being lost. The story begins at menarche, in the blue hour, when she's alone and barefoot in a field, bleeding onto fresh, white flowers. She returns, wearing a white dress, to her narrow white room, with a white bed, white desk, white sheets, and a white mirror, holding a blood-stained white flower.

Her grandmother, a pale woman of ambiguous age, dressed in white, enters the kitchen while the young girl twirls around and around, eating bread. The young girl clasps her hands in prayer.

"Grandma," she whispers. "The actors have arrived."

She removes a silver earring from her ear, dangles it over a teacup.

"Are you playing with your earring, child?" asks the grandmother.

The young girl clasps her hands again. "I am not a child anymore."

"At the age of 13. Just like your mother." The grandmother begins to pray for the young girl, for the earrings she has found, forsaken by the young girl's mother, her daughter, who is now dead. The young girl wonders what the earrings know that her grandmother cannot teach her. Partly attached to her mother in the afterlife, she longs to wear them for eternity, these immortal earrings.

"Is there some secret in these earrings?" asks the young girl, smiling. She runs to the window, where, through the frame, a performance is beginning to take place. "Grandma, it's the actors!"

She can practically taste their fingertips-of-rose, soft-as-suede fragrance. A flower lounges, smokes cigarettes, and eats fresh petal salads.

> *Khaos* I was born a flower. My sisters are flowers. My mother is a flower, and her mother is a flower, and her mother is a flower. I am pregnant and will soon give birth to a baby flower. Cue entrance music.

Karma enters. There's music and smiling and waving. Air kisses.

> *Karma* Hi Daughter.
> *Khaos* Hi Mother.

They dissolve into long awkward laughter.

> *Khaos* Mom comes in wearing bright colors, bug-eyed sunglasses, and hair spiked like a dryer ball. I tell her that she looks like a butterfly in electric shock. When she kisses me her face rubs off on my collar, I can't tell if it's foundation or her literal

skin flaking off after years of chemical treatments, all over the house!

Karma Khaos, that is so rude. Try my style for a day—just try it. You'll feel younger, wiser, more confident—!

Karma takes a power stance and gets horizontal, flipping through the latest tabloid at the top of her stack of tabloids, the pages flying up and down like the wings of a stunned butterfly. Khaos narrows her eyes and takes an extra-long drag of her cigarette.

Khaos Ugh, Mom. I think that's an exhausting idea. It's so… litigative. All anyone wants to do is catch me in some kind of lie. Self-definition can be sooo… limiting?

Karma —Maybe even a bit more *likeable*! Think of it this way, Khaos, there are tools to the self, as the self is a tool. You have all the tools you need to escape yourself—and to reinvent yourself in a charismatic and empowered package. My mantra is always: Confidence Is Capital.

Karma grabs the cigarette out of Khaos's mouth and throws it onto the floor.

Karma Step one: Don't smoke. It's an ideological *virus*.

Setting: an apartment in New York. Mother lives there, and Daughter has dropped out of school and moved to the city. Daughter asks for a place to stay. Mother tells her she can stay at her place if Daughter will do her the favor of making a new copy of her keys—she can't find them.

Daughter *[on the phone]* Am I staying at your apartment alone?

Mother *[on the phone]* I want you to be comfortable! Have the place to
yourself.

Daughter doesn't press the question of why someone wouldn't have keys to
their own home. There's no answer that would be any more believable than
any other. Daughter hangs up the phone, walks the miasmic halls of Penn
Station, and rides the C train downtown to Spring Street, where Mother
lives next door to Sandra Bullock.

Daughter enters Mother's one-bedroom apartment, where inside,
everything is packed up as if she is about to move: The beds are stripped
and everything's boxed, cleaned, and folded. In her fridge is a six-pack
of Corona, nothing else: no grody sauce stains or half-used bottles of
condiments, not even olives. Mother never cooks at home anymore. Her job
has something to do with wining and dining and no matter how many times
she has tried to explain this to Daughter, Daughter never has any idea what
she does or why her meals are always being taken care of.

One of the many aphorisms Mother loves to announce is that—

Mother I live an outside life now, where I never, ever have to use my
kitchen!

Daughter's entrance should repeat itself again and again, with more
redaction, until she walks into the apartment and everything is bare, even
the toilet has been de-installed. The walls are see-through and the apartment
is slowly disappearing into glass, slowly leaking.

Daughter I open the window to the fire escape and smoke a cigarette.
I look down into Sandra Bullock's courtyard, and at the
figures moving around in the windows. My mom insists that
she lives there, but so far, I have never, ever seen her.

Mom has left some wilted white roses on her kitchen counter. She always says that a classy woman has fresh roses in the home, that they make a room feel complete and that studies say they boost your mood. She buys white roses and gigantic white candles even though my grandmother would always tell her that white is the color of death. She'll buy the whitest, purest, dirtless, creaseless roses. She thinks that any smudge on anything expresses touch, and touch expresses grime, and grime is gross.

Don't mess with my serenity, she'll say.

She wants to live in a blank slate.

A crisp catalog world.

Maybe that is why she could never bring herself to go home, where all of the grimy, creepy-crawly truths lie, refusing to be forgotten. Refusing to die.

When I was growing up, and I would stay with her on the weekends, we would spend all afternoon at the movies, paying one entrance fee and moving from theater to theater, movie to movie. Often in the darkened room we would fall asleep. Sometimes I imagine that we are both still young, still in a cinema, and we are both sleeping, both dreaming that we live in a beautiful house with no sense of attachment, where everything is new, beautiful, designed, where there is no clutter, where nothing breaks, where we can't become homesick for a place we can never return to.

Daughter looks through Mother's boxes and finds: makeup, dried flowers, candles, bloody silk pillowcases, and bills addressed to Bill and Kara Shaw. Daughter assumes that Mother is the addressee Kara Shaw, though she goes by many names: her legal name, the American name she has given herself, or sometimes a fake name altogether. Daughter does not know who Bill Shaw is, but she doesn't think that Mother has remarried, though she's not entirely sure. Daughter assumes that Mother was pretending to be his wife, because she's done this a lot, maybe to hide an affair, maybe to avoid questioning, or maybe just because she likes the fantasy of it: being a wife at home with her husband. Or maybe she likes to be someone who doesn't exist at all… someone who can just disappear. Daughter tries googling Bill Shaw's name, but that, of course, is futile.

Daughter turns on the TV. She watches a film entirely situated in a hotel along the Mekong River, the border between Thailand and Laos, where a filmmaker directs rehearsals of a film he has written called *Ecstasy Garden*, in which a mother and daughter play versions of themselves: The mother, a hungry ghost, slowly eats her daughter at the height of her daughter's love for someone else. The daughter's spirit follows her lost love from continent to continent, but the further her spirit drifts, the more she is ensnared in her mother's web. Mother and daughter are trapped in the world of the hotel for the duration of the film, backgrounded by an acoustic guitar and the Mekong River, both which lure us into a poly-temporal state. "Mommy," says the daughter, laying with her mother in bed. "After all these years, it's so painful. Where are you? Can I meet you?"

"I'm always in my room," says the mother. "It's been 600 years now. I'm not so far from Earth. I used to believe in God. I used to believe in something that gave a sweet aroma to flesh and set me free. I'm disgusted by this savagery.

"I hate that my life turned out this way," she cries. "I hate it."

"Go to bed, mom," says the daughter. "We'll be together. Our memories are one."

Khaos Mom has redesigned the house 807 times, each time her social status changes. We are sitting at the latest table, which is an old fridge turned on its side. I am still wrapped in my blanket and slowly eating a fresh petal salad that I have craved for as long as I can remember.

Karma   Do you like the décor changes I've made to the house, honey?

Khaos   Truthfully, I don't think they're *significant* enough.

Karma   *Significant* enough?

Khaos   To wake me up out of this crotch-drying banality!

There is an awkward silence as the two flowers ignore the outburst, eat their salads slowly and watch the screens on the surfaces of the walls, where a reclusive mother has trapped her daughter in her mansion for 25 years, and they spend all day wandering in and out of the rooms and performing to an imagined audience, singing, changing and rearranging their clothes, arguing and recalling the past surrounded by cats and raccoons and the artifacts of the upper class from which they've exiled themselves. "I never feel right in this place," shouts the daughter, in one scene. "It's boring, boring, boring here!" In another, she gazes longingly at her garden, commenting, "That was the original living room. You know, maybe it will go back to a kitchen now. Though the washing machine was always put in the maid's dining room. It's very difficult to keep the line between the past and the present, you know what I mean? It's awfully difficult." Their house is named after the color of the dunes, the cement garden walls, the sea mist, the fading of something once bright and lively.

Khaos   The kitchen, though. I *love* what you've done to this kitchen. The lighting is great, flat and even. Flaw-less. Literally. I think if you can have a good kitchen, it doesn't really matter where you live. You never have to go outside.

Karma   Oh no. *Outside?* No. Why would you do that? We're making memories!

Karma opens the door of the fridge-that-is-now-a-table, which turns it into a kind of couch. She poses for a photo taken somewhere by a camera implanted in a pore of a surface's skin. Khaos joins her and focuses on a screen, where, in a dusty, desolate Southern California desert town, an eternal child arrives mysteriously and moves in with her new co-worker, who is everything she is not: self-absorbed, sexual, and deluded, an isolated extrovert who is obsessed with adoration and the consumer goods that it promises to bring to her. Over the course of the film, with the blankness of an alien performing intuitive humanness, the childlike girl dons her roommate's identity like a mask. Then swallows her. Brooding on the couch, Khaos wonders, am I really so porous that someone could just bleed into me? She shapes this secret concern into a friendlier façade.

Daughter Digging through her closet, I find silk bundled in a corner, and shaking it out, discover it is an old áo dài, faded and wrinkly. Hanging it over the door, I lay down and stare at the blank, white walls. I light a white candle. When she had first moved to New York, when she was thirty-five and I was fifteen, she took the time to decorate her first apartment with huge, blown-up headshots of herself. She was modeling for QVC, and was the spokesperson for CBS, where her line was, "The address is CBS—welcome home!"—smiling so hard one dimple appeared in her cheek.

She was really proud of those ads: being the face of a national corporation. Everyone watched CBS. I was proud, too. I videotaped the commercial and would watch and rewind, watch and rewind the video recording until it grew silvery ribbons of static. It looked like glitter and I loved the image more for it, the way it wore its scars like a beautiful coat. I am always loving the wrong thing.

After that first apartment she lived in three different apartments on three corners of West Broadway and Prince. She couldn't imagine living anywhere but Soho. She loved Soho—she loved shopping, window-shopping, and she loved seeing celebrities. They were real to her. They were intimate. They were her gossip, her friends, her role models. She dressed like them, followed their beauty regimens, their secret skin remedies, their weight-loss products. The last time I saw her, she was wearing shorts, a T-shirt, a Rolex, and a hat pulled down low, like she was hiding from the paparazzi.

We were a sight. Me in a giant fur, runs in my tights. She with long, fake lashes.

The bigness of everything blankets itself over Daughter in a haze. Swaddled in tulle, she dances and waves her hands around in the air. She imagines shrinking the world down to the size of a tiny compact mirror, so that she is a little Polly Pocket in the family plot.

Enter Mother, wearing her wrinkled silk áo dài.

Daughter Hi Mother.
Mother Hi Daughter.

Mother and Daughter sit on the couch and stare at the screen, at white-clad schoolgirls who embark on a picnic and are swallowed by a rock. Time stops at the top of the rock. Four girls break off from the pack. They hold hands through the scrub. They remove their stockings, their shoes, their hats. As though possessed, they are swallowed up by the rock and never return. A young girl with glasses, beholding her luminous oneness against the rest of her schoolmates gathered below, wonders, "Whatever can those people be doing down there, like a lot of ants? A surprising number of human beings are without purpose. Though it is probable they are performing some function unknown to themselves." The girls lay down on the rock. Flies and ants gather at their bare feet. The rock rumbles and watches them from above. "I feel awful," shouts one girl. "When are we going home? *When are we going home?!*" The rest of the girls continue to ascend the rock, unresponsive, their ribbons askew. The girl screams. They cannot find the road home. Whether through the shadow of formative myth ("I named you Peter because you are a rock," "I cried, and crying, grieved for my mother"), Daughter, too, finds herself pulled into this strange new vista of reality, where there haven't been visitors for a long, long time.

Mother Daughter, what are you going to do about getting out of the house. You need to make a plan to get out of the house, get married, and do something with your life! Or are you just going to stay inside and be a boring whore?!

Daughter *[staring at the TV]* Mother, staying inside is safe. I can think of nothing more disorienting than the dull roar of the unknown.

Mother That sounds like depression.

Mother takes Daughter's temperature, then tosses the thermometer away and spritzes Daughter with rose water.

Mother My diagnosis is that you have very sensitive skin. You should never try bee venom face masks. You should live in a world with soft corners. You should never use sharp knives.

Daughter Never?

Mother *Ever.*

Mother takes off her áo dài and reveals another sort of hip and sexy outfit underneath, dances and waves her hands around in the air, then finds a door in the wall and disappears.

Daughter The next day I go to check the mail. I find an unsealed envelope, with a rent bill four months past due. There are four of these. I pack a bowl and take a hit to walk around the neighborhood and meet my mom for lunch. This time, I will really ask her why she doesn't have a copy of her own keys and what's the story with the rent. At the front door of the building, the super appears. 'Where's your mom,' she asks. I am agitated and unresponsive. 'She's four months behind rent,' she tells me. I reach for the door, trying to perform cool and confident even though the weed is hitting my head. 'You can't stay here,' she calls after me. 'Your mom's behind rent, you can't just *stay here!*'

Scene 2

Setting: Hotel in Miami, where Mother and Daughter are on a family vacation to celebrate Thanksgiving.

Daughter   Let me begin by saying that I am resistant and skeptical. Every family vacation we have ever been on has ended in disaster. She will blow up on me publicly, or call the whole vacation off and make a huge thing out of standing at the front desk booking plane tickets to go home and cancelling her room reservation, while I will spend the afternoon trapped on the lobby couch, watching her glare at me and the whole world. What she wants out of this whole scheme is an elaborate, groveling apology, proof that she has a devoted admirer in me, and eventually, I will crack and perform this role to keep the peace and not waste time. But wasting time is inevitable. And so is her doubt in me. I am not devoted. I have avoided family vacations for years.

And she has avoided Thanksgivings. She has stopped living in apartments and is living in hotels, where she doesn't even have a kitchen. We always meet in public space—bars and restaurants and the like. From one award-winning art-directed space to another we spend our time together. Now we are in Miami. South Beach.

Karma unlocks the door and enters the room.

Khaos	Where have you been? I've been looking everywhere for you.
Karma	*Where* have you been looking?
Khaos	Your part of the house, find-my-phone, all of my social networks…
Karma	I was just outside, honey.
Khaos	I don't get it, Mom. You feel like a stranger to me. I know we're busy, but we're still family. You feel so far away.
Karma	Why do I have to be a totally transparent person? Can't I just keep a part of my life to myself?
Khaos	Why would you want to do that?
Karma	I don't want to live under any rules?
Khaos	Rules give me purpose, relief—like a massage.
Karma	Oh my god, Khaos. Have you ever come across anyone more desperate than yourself? You need to make a plan to get out of the house and have your baby.
Khaos	*[grabbing a knife to file her nails]* Yeah, I'm gonna do that tomorrow.

They sit quietly for a very long time, each trying to think of something interesting to say to the other in the deep internal folds of their shared room, eyes glued to a screen, where two teenage girls bond over a history of childhood isolation. They develop an intense friendship and fantasy world, a fortress in a green field where human creatures are made of clay. "We saw a gateway through the clouds," says one of the girls. "Everything was full of peace and bliss. We then realized we have the key!" One day, when the pressure of their family lives makes them nearly explode, the girls use their keys to bury themselves deep in their world of clay. The order of their lives begins to dissolve, and as it dissolves, they escape again and again, and the deeper their world of clay, the deeper their anger.

Daughter We meet at the Miami airport. She is excited to take me to our hotel. Super hip, super fancy, she keeps saying. Everyone wanting to stay there. She's excited to show me Collins Avenue, what she calls 'The Strip.' 'Everyone walks down The Strip,' she recounts, 'trying to get you into their bar.' We check in, walk out of the hotel, and get dumped onto The Strip, where one establishment seems absolutely indistinguishable from the next and touristy. 'Isn't this exciting?' she asks. She loves to show me what's hip, to show me she knows what's what, that she's finally made something of herself.

'But what's outside The Strip?' I ask her. She says she doesn't know. 'It just feels like a road with tons of restaurants and bars and stores,' I gripe, 'like the set of a city, but where's the real city?' 'There's nothing beyond here,' she assures me. We approach the concierge with our battle of the wills. 'Where's the real Miami?' I ask them. I'm beginning to feel ridiculous, and desperate. They direct me to Collins Avenue. 'Something more authentic,' I clarify. My mom shares a knowing look with the concierge: Baby, this *is* authentic.

Later that night, after walking the exhaustive length of Collins Avenue, Mother and Daughter return to the hotel. They enter their room and inside, everything is packed up as if Mother is about to leave: The beds are stripped, and everything is boxed, cleaned, and folded. Her luggage is zipped up and neatly perched at the foot of the bed. The fridge is bare, the TV is stacked on its side against the wall, and the furniture has been removed. The curtains have been taken off their rods and left in piles on the floor. Mother reaches for a suitcase and twirls it on its wheels.

Mother	I'm leaving. Sayōnara, so long, auf weidersehen, adieu!
Daughter	You're leaving me here alone?
Mother	I'm going to stay with a friend in the city. I want you to be comfortable and have fun.
Daughter	Why don't you stay here and have fun with me?
Mother	I wanted to save some money to treat you. Have the whole place to yourself! Order room service. Order bottle service. Order Direct TV. Order a facial. Order pizza. Order a velvet robe.

Like the perfect odd couple, Mother and her suitcase find the door in the wall and leave. Daughter is jealous. She turns on the TV and flips to *House*, where Prof, Kung Fu, Melody, and Fantasy dig through layers and layers of bedding but do not find Sweet. They find scraps of her, though: her apron, her bra, a naked doll.

"Something smells funny," comments Prof.

Melody holds up Sweet's underwear.

"I saw it!" shouts Fantasy, but no one is listening. "The mats and sheets leaping on her like beasts!"

The channel changes. A woman lies on a bed wrapped in white sheets. Her friend unwraps her. "It's nice to be home," her friend whispers. Her friend rolls her up again in the sheets, rolls her off the bed. "Die! Die! Die!"

Her friend lies in bed. The girl rolls her up in a red sheet, whispering, "I'M ON FIRE, YOU'RE ON FIRE, WE'RE ON FIRE."

Her friend rolls the girl up in a black sheet. She whispers, "Can you feel how volatile life is?"

The friend rolls the girl up in a blue sheet. "What'll become of us?"

The girl rolls her friend up in a black sheet. "There's no proof at all."

The girl lays splayed on a black sheet, whispering, "I'm lying here. Just imagine if it weren't me." Her friend dumps a handful of scissors onto the bed, cuts into the sheet, cuts into the girl's clothes.

"Too much!" says the girl. Grabbing a pair of scissors, she cuts off her friend's arm, then cuts off her own head.

> *Khaos* I spritz myself 100 times a day with rose water. The chemical interactions of rose water and pheromone create new auras, new rings, new forms of desire. I was brought to this house by my mother, and she was looking for a better life. The more I tried to enter, the further away the door.

Karma enters: There's music and smiling and waving. Whole chunks of the architecture fall away.

> *Karma* You know what, Khaos? You should have a house party.
>
> *Khaos* That's the last thing I want.
>
> *Karma* Why not? It's a huge, beautiful house.
>
> *Khaos* I just don't want people in my space, you know? Messing it up. Looking at me and calling me a sperm whale. If I wanted people to stare at me and judge me then I would just go outside and get a fro-yo. And I would, but every time I try to step outside, everything becomes warped and wobbly.
>
> *Karma* Well, Khaos, unfortunately, the world is not designed for stilettos.
>
> *Khaos* Fuck a duck.

They grab two enormous petal salads from their pristine white kitchen and shake them.

> *Khaos* Where does this food even come from?
>
> *Karma* Lord knows. Let's say grace.

A pause while they arrange themselves. They hold hands in a circle around the kitchen table.

    Khaos Long live this New Flesh.
    Karma Thank you for our Family. Under the light of play and pretend may we act in brand new ways.
    Khaos Amen.
    Karma Amen.

Mother enters the hotel room in a rush and lays two vouchers down on the table, addressed to Khanh Nguyen.

    Mother Get whatever you want. They spelled my name wrong, but don't worry about it. I didn't bother to correct them.
  Daughter I recognize the name: I'd seen it on her computer, and sometimes on e-mails she'd sent me. I know that it is not her name, or even a misspelling of her name, because it is a man's name. I know that a man named Khanh Nguyen is paying for the room. I am sure that I have never met Khanh Nguyen.

Mother's nose begins to bleed. Daughter hands her a tissue. Mother dabs at her nose, her eyes.

  Daughter Mother, who pays for you to live in this way?
    Mother In what way? I struggle. For thirty-five years I have raised a child who has needed constant care. Do you remember when you were young that I drove for four hours every other weekend to see you? We would stay in hotels and I would take you shopping and to eat the best food, that other daughters would *die to eat!*

Daughter When I was young your visits meant that we would drive to places that would never arrive. We would spend all day in the temporary space, waiting for the room upgrade, waiting for a table, waiting for our turn at the putt-putt course, waiting for you to calm down, waiting for me to calm down. When it was all over you would take me home and cry for hours while you said goodbye, while I waited for you to stop crying. Everything was always a crisis. Mostly I waited to be old enough to be in charge of myself. To not wait anymore. Now the waiting is done. I am no longer a child. And you are no longer a child.

Mother What else could you possibly want? I gave you everything I had to give: duck liver mousse, cobb salads, oysters, every specialty-of-the-house. I gave you my youth. Now I want it back and you resent me for it. You dare ask who paid for these things: I PAID. I PAID. I PAID. I PAID.

Mother unzips her outfit and reveals a hip and sexy layer underneath, then finds a door in the wall and leaves.

Daughter I go downstairs to the bar, where I charge the hell out of Khanh Nguyen's card. Should I feel sorry for him? NO. Why should money vibrate with the white noise of guilt? Sure, every charge is a sacrifice made by every party involved, but it is also my personal revenge. Every swipe screams: I LOST THINGS TOO AND NOW I WANT THEM BACK—I PAID, I PAID, I PAID, I PAID! The bar is by the pool, and the pool is surrounded by lush, white, gauzy beds: WHITE, THE COLOR OF WEALTH AND DEATH. SWIPE, SWIPE, SWIPE. Which is why these rooms cost every cent that they do. Except that on this Thanksgiving night, the hotel, pool, bar, beds, and rooms are empty. SWIPE, SWIPE, SWIPE. Whoever decided the unspoken laws of our transactional relationship? Did I ever get to have a say in it? What did I deserve? What did she owe me? SWIPE, SWIPE, SWIPE. I drink whiskey in the empty hotel bar, where the infinity pool drips into a room in which I am lost.

Karma and Khaos eat salads and stare at one another warily. There is a leaky faucet dripping.

> *Khaos* MOM, please fix that leaky faucet. This broken home makes me *soooo*... TIRED!!!
>
> *Karma* Khaos, this is making me really sad… all I ever did was bring you to Paradise.
>
> *Khaos* *[lighting up]* Ma, I've got my own methods for filling the void.

Scene 3

Setting: New York, The Standard Hotel. Daughter has made a series of dramatic life moves that haven't panned into anything of interest and has no money whatsoever and nowhere to live. Mother is staying at The Standard Hotel and invites Daughter to stay with her.

Mother Don't worry about the money, my company's paying for it! We can do face masks and go dancing and stay up all night long, talking and bonding.

Daughter I stay with her at The Standard Hotel for three weeks. I barely ever see her. I start working at a restaurant, then go out after. Since she says she has clients in New York and Asia, she is up intermittently day and night. In the middle of the night I wake up to her clicking softly on her blackberry, her fake lashes, her earrings, lit up by the glow of the blue light.

I'm working the door at a popular Vietnamese restaurant, where it seems that everyone in New York's Asian-American fashion scene hangs out. It's a hot summer, and coming in to work, my co-workers and I open all the windows, blast Italo Disco and squirt big Sriracha bottles into little Sriracha bottles, big hoisin sauce bottles into little hoisin sauce bottles, bopping our heads to the beat. Then we slide the bottles onto each individual table, treating the aisles between the tiny tables like our runway, our dance floor. After closing we push all the tables to the walls and friends stay behind to dance, and the chef makes big midnight dinners served with big bottles of wine and Japanese whiskey, and we put out little plates with wet napkins to tap out cigarette ash, and sometimes very late at night we wander to Jane Street where we dance on tables and lay across velvet couches, or around the corner to Broome Street, and up the three flights of stairs to the Chinese karaoke bar, where we sing Olivia Newton-John's 'Magic' every time: 'Have to believe we are magic… nothing can stand in our way…' I meet everybody in the scene, which they call a family. We stretch our radiance through the sweltering Manhattan summer.

I love the candlelight and the street lights and the sirens that throw blue and red quarters of light across everyone's faces. I play songs like 'Bandiera Bianca' and instinctively diners groove to the beat. Joy. I have long, dark hair and wear all black, with black lipstick, lining my eyes in blue and silver. I think, everything's okay, it's finally cool. Everything's cool, don't trip out. I never trip out, and for a short while I have a hell of a lot of fun, being invited into this world, going dancing till dawn, feeling like I own the streets, the door, the crowd, dissolving into the dazzle. I wear it like a beautiful coat. It almost feels like home.

Karma and Khaos sit around the kitchen table. Khaos is smoking a cigarette, carefully shaking her petal salad.

Khaos How sad. A single tear cuts a clean line down my makeup.

Real tears flow, turning Khaos's dark mascara into raccoon eyes.

Daughter Then one day, my mom calls me at work. 'I have to leave *today*,' she says. Urgent as always. 'Work wants me to move to Hong Kong *tomorrow*,' she says. 'I don't know if I'll get to see you before I leave, but I love you.'

That's the last night I spend at the hotel. When I come back from work, I let myself into the room and inside, everything is packed up. The beds are stripped and her clothes are in boxes by the window, looking out over a glassy view of smashed up skyscrapers and lights. The fridge is bare; the TV is stacked on its side against the wall. The furniture has been removed. The curtains have been taken off their rods and left in piles on the floor. I look through her boxes, thinking about how much I hate most of her clothes, how cheaply they were made and how much they cost. I feel like I'm walking around in an unbalanced room. I pick up a shirt and shake it out.

Dust and cells fly everywhere, glomming back together into Mother's glittery form.

> *Mother* [*extending a glittery hand*] My baby.
> *Daughter* Mother, do you love your clothes more than me?
> *Mother* I love my clothes—they are peaceful.
> *Daughter* I have looked for you my whole life like you were a shirt. I have let the shirt guide me.

Mother wiggles out of her glittery outfit and throws it onto the pile, revealing something sort of hip and sexy underneath. She finds the door in the wall and leaves.

> *Daughter* After she leaves, her clothes start rapidly turning into trash. As quickly as I can I take fur, necklaces, bras, and leather.

Then I leave, too. Whatever I don't take, I leave behind, and she leaves behind, except for her credit card.

Response shot: In the sealed-off room, the clothes go limp and lifeless and prepare for a new life, having lost the body that lived in them. On the TV screen, flipped on its side and nearly mute, a failed Hollywood actress has cast her dream-self in an old Hollywood film, fashioning her character's narrative so as to alleviate her own self-pity and her guilt over killing the woman she loves. She dreams her lover is a damsel in distress she controls like a doll. Throughout the film, she falls asleep many times. Perhaps she rehearses a self and puts it to sleep, rehearses a self and puts it to sleep, so that she is many possible selves who are sleeping. In this particular moment, she wakes up suddenly, sits up in her bed and decides, *I can act!*

Khaos Do you even have a personality, or is it just bad acting?

The television flips to close-ups of a young girl looking into the camera blinking vacantly. Blinking pensively. Blinking and thinking. Blinking for a moment. Blinking and looking far, far away. Thinking far, faraway things, with faraway eyes. Recounting what happened. Recounting the way things were. Recounting her sides of things. Recounting in a slow-moving portrait. A living picture. The camera watches. Watches her eat, smoke, drink, swallow, breathe, talk, smile, bite her nails, play with her teeth. She talks to the camera directly, sometimes, or sometimes she glances directly at the camera while interacting with her world. Sometimes she avoids eye contact completely. Sometimes she breaks character and reveals the line between her "real" and "artificial" character. Sometimes the camera backs up and reveals all the artifice: the apparatus of the set, the grammar of ideologies, the vernacular of her world, and the methods of storytelling that make the viewer feel as though the young girl is just a doll in the viewer's personal game of make-believe, the story she tells herself.

> *Khaos* *[tapping on a camera in the wall and whispering]* I know my
> mother's in there…
>
> *Daughter* I have made a series of bad choices and need her help to get
> back on track. I need a navigational device in a world that is
> big and unfamiliar. So I let myself into her building and up
> into her one-bedroom apartment, where everything is packed
> up as if she's about to move: The beds are stripped, and
> everything is boxed, cleaned, and folded. The curtains have
> been taken off their rods and placed into plastic. The kitchen
> faucet has been ripped from its fixture and placed on its side.
> The door to the kitchen has been taken off its hinges and
> leaned against the wall. Walking through the-space-in-the-
> wall-that-is-not-a-door, I turn the corner into her bathroom,
> where even the toilet has been de-installed, packed. A thin
> layer of water covers the floor, though I don't understand how,
> given that everything that pours water has been taken apart.
> The room smells scummy, like a gym. I dip my finger into the
> water and write CLEAN ME on the wall, as a note-to-self.

Mother lets herself into the apartment, wearing her wrinkly áo dài, her
long, dark hair stick-straight.

> *Mother* *[waving and throwing glitter in the air]* There she is, Miss
> American Dream!
>
> *Daughter* Don't you mean Miss America?
>
> *Mother* I meant America's Sweetheart.
>
> *Daughter* Why is she gracing me with her presence?
>
> *Mother* To properly say goodbye.

Mother grabs two bottles of Corona from the fridge and pours beer into two champagne flutes, handing one to Daughter.

> *Daughter* Mother, are you going to take anything with you when you go to Hong Kong?
>
> *Mother* My credit card.
>
> *Daughter* You don't want a picture, you don't want a candle, you don't want a mug, you don't want a memory?
>
> *Mother* No silly—I can always go to the store and get a new one!

They sip their glasses slowly, noses to the bottom of the flute. The head is a bell. The water is slowly rising. It is at the ankles.

> *Daughter* She smiles. There's a tiny gap in the side of her mouth, to the left of the left canine. I've never noticed it before. It makes her appear different to me. Awkward, but carnal. A tiny gap she has been performing with for her entire life. I put a chill rhythmic beat on the boombox, feel it in my core, and face her absence directly.

Mother gives a speech over the techno beat.

> *Mother* When you were born, I was just twenty, living my life, having fun. And then I met your daddy. When you're just twenty, you don't really know who you are, or what you want to do with your life. I was just a girl younger than you are now, and when you were born my mother said, 'Karma will give you a bad daughter, because you were a bad daughter.' And she was right. It wasn't easy being a mother. My greatest joy has been teaching you things that

only I can teach you. What is the greatest thing that I have taught you?

Daughter pauses in reflection, taking a sip of her Corona. She shuffles in the water, which has reached her knees. Finally she says:

Daughter How to make things perfect in an imperfect reality!

Mother And what else?

Daughter My fire > the maternal ecology!

Mother May you burn, burn, burn the world down while you're young, Miss Baby of Miss American Dream.

Daughter I am angry. All I have ever wanted in my life was someone in my corner. Facing her, I smile cruelly, display my fangs. I say, Mother, why are you moving to Hong Kong?

Mother It's a secret. It's all one big secret.

Daughter What will I do without you?

Mother Ugggh, don't you think if I knew the answer I would have told you by now?

Mother changes the song on the boombox. Using her beer bottle as a mic, she begins to sing a lullaby.

Daughter That's when I recognize that she's wearing the áo dài she wore to my uncle's wedding, at Galaxy Night Club. Instinctively I prepare myself for 'The Rose,' the song I know most intimately, the one she practiced for months and months with her brothers, while vacuuming the carpets, in the car, while putting me to sleep. By heart I know her inhale, how she finds her low guttural register and opens her mouth to sing: 'Some say love, it is a river…' I remember how every time she'd finish the song she'd hold her breath to see if I'd fallen asleep yet, and I would hold my breath to see if she'd inhale and begin the song again. I'd know that as soon as I'd fall asleep she would leave, so when I'd hear the rustle of her getting out of bed, I'd open my eyes to tell her no, I had not fallen asleep yet, so she would lay down again and stay, breathe in and begin to sing again.

But this time I do not close my eyes and she does not sing the song again. This time she leaves, dropping the bottle to the floor, taking off her áo dài to reveal a sexy outfit underneath, floating away via long, river-bound strands of hair.

The water has now reached the tip of the CLEAN ME mark on the wall, then completely washes the words away as it rises, drifting and accumulating and flowing until it surrounds Daughter, her long black strands of hair lifted around her head like spaghetti, like petals on a sea anemone, turning the whole room into a fishbowl. She stares at the window, trying to make out what's glass, and what's beyond-glass. But why wonder when she always ends up back here?

The girls stand around Fantasy and talk as if she's not even there. Fantasy SEES things, but no one really SEES Fantasy. Fantasy might not even be real. In her head all of the time, she is not a very trusted guide to reality. And doesn't that get to you sometimes, Fantasy? Do you even understand that this is being done to you? *THEY ARE TELLING YOU THAT YOUR REALITY IS NOT REAL.*

Kung Fu says to Prof, "Things are going just as Fantasy imagined. What do you think, Prof?"

"I can't tell you," Prof replies. "Because I'm not completely sure of it yet." The camera passes between them, back and forth. Back and forth. Fantasy is silent. "Besides," Prof concludes, "Fantasy would pass out."

Poor Fantasy. She's always the witness. No one believes her because of her archetype. "All of us will disappear," she frets. "I'm sure of it."

"Don't worry!" say Prof, Kung Fu, and Melody. "Your love, Mr. Togo, is coming! He's a man after all. He can help us!" Fantasy pictures Mr. Togo on a horse galloping towards her in a prince's coat, down a grassy hillside.

"Oh, my lovely Princess Fantasy!" he shouts, in English.

Fantasy runs towards him in a girlish white dress and a tiara like she has seen stars do in the movies, arms outstretched. "My lovely teacher!"

"I helped you! I love you!" he shouts, in English.

"END," says a voice, in English. "No—The End!" says another, in English. The End flashes across the screen. The image jump cuts with a black screen while the voice shouts "The End" again and again, violently.

THE END

THE END

THE END

THE END

Daughter After she leaves, I touch my toes. I stare at my hands underwater. I smash all of the empty bottles and champagne flutes against the walls. I toss coins and watch them drag themselves down through the great blue Jell-O, then I swim and pick them all up like a champ. I learn new methods for breathing. They recalibrate my heart and my rage. Swimming to a shard of glass on the floor, I gently cut out all of my mother's things and throw them in the trash. Hong Kong is far, I think. If there's one thing she could've left behind, it should've been a key.

It gets a little suffocating waiting underwater with nowhere to go for years and years. Swimming to the window, I press my face to the glass and try to lift it. I knock, kick, and scream. On several occasions I see Sandra Bullock, down below. 'Sandra!' I yell. Bubbles escape from my mouth. 'Sandra! Come save me!' But Sandra does not come to the window. No one does.

Act 2

Scene 1

Khaos is chain-smoking, lying in bed on top of many soft pillows. Prof, Kung Fu, Melody, and Fantasy find Gorgeous in Auntie's room, emerging from the mirror wearing a white nightgown. They follow her in procession down the winding staircase, where Gorgeous considers the thought, "I don't blame Fantasy. I understand."

"Mr. Togo is coming soon. Be patient!" Melody exclaims.

"Mr. Togo?" Gorgeous is confused.

"In a buggy… but he acts like he's flying a plane."

"A plane?"

The soundtrack plays the sound of a plane and of shooting, as though this conversation is cross-fading through the memory of the house, as if old memories can be resuscitated in new bodies. The camera shakes and voices echo as if inhabiting the eyes of a ghost. Making her way to the bottom of the stairway, she calls the police while the girls hover around her. The phone talks back to her: HELP ME! HELP ME! HELP ME! Like a zombie, Gorgeous cradles the phone to her ear and hears nothing. Hanging up the phone, she shrugs and says to her friends, "It's out of order." For the first time in the entire film, there's no background music. Everything is quiet.

Gorgeous leaves the girls to look for help, closing them behind the heavy front door. The windows fly shut. "I'll be back!" says Auntie. Freaked out, they turn around, see nothing but a huge, swelling space.

"She is the house!" the girls scream, pounding their fists on the wall. "Take us with you!"

Khaos All day, I watch *House* in bed, and I watch my belly grow bigger. I am afraid of losing my youth. I am afraid of losing possibility. I don't know what is going to happen to my vagina. I don't know what to do with a baby.

A Sister enters, takes a huge puff of her cigarette and blows it at Khaos's face.

Sister Get out of the bed, Khaos.
Khaos I'm taking an in-the-bed day, Sister! Self-care is self-love.

Another Sister walks in.

Sister Get out of the bed, Khaos. This is *juvenile*.
Khaos Ugggggh, I'm pregnant.
Sister Lots of people are pregnant. Get over yourself.

Another Sister walks in, smoking.

Sister Khaos, you need to get a grip, get over it, and make a plan to get out of the house and have your baby.
Sister She hasn't made a plan yet? She's about to explode!
Sister She's organized her outfit and makeup. She says that she wants her baby's first thought to be that she's the most beautiful woman in the world.

The Sisters are plucking long strands of their petals to make a salad together, each lighting cigarettes off of another's cigarette butt. After filling a giant bowl, they each grab a section of its lip and toss it together, singing, cigs hanging out of their mouths. Khaos turns the volume up to drown out the sound of her sisters singing.

Huddling around the piano, the girls attempt to piece together the clues. "Shouldn't Gorgeous be back by now?" Fantasy asks. Prof hears humming from far away and perks up. "She's back!" Prof and Kung Fu run upstairs. Fantasy stays behind, unable to return to her innocence. She shakes Melody, who responds by holding up her fingers, which are slowly disappearing into the glow. Melody thinks, it makes sense that the piano should want to swallow me, simmering me in its bloody stew: After all, the piano is the primary instrument of the house's voice. The piano is a beautiful instrument but needs a human hand to *PLAY IT*.

> *Daughter* I have been trapped in this apartment for seventeen years. I am a prisoner here. Everything around me is drowning. The flowers are drowning. The faucets are growing algae and grime. When I look at the broken bottles I see a silent scream.

Grandmother Z opens the door in the wall without knocking. Seventeen years' worth of water rushes out like a dam breaking. She enters.

> *Grandmother Z* [*in a high, cheery Transatlantic accent*] Hallo! War will come again. You must do several things: Get your German passport renewed. Get cash. Pocket a nest egg. Learn German, or better yet, Swedish. No, German—the literature is better. Learn to fight. Learn what to do if someone tries to assault you. Learn a manual job—plumbing, or anything in health care, is good. Learn to grow your own food. Learn to jog. Jog frequently. Sweat—it gets rid of the toxins, raises endorphins. Learn to do your taxes. Begin to practice your gunshot. Pray it will not be brutal. Oh—most importantly—get out of the house. Today.
>
> *Daughter* Today?!

Grandmother Z Ja! Fate loves the fearless! Get dressed.

Daughter I get up and go to the closet where I had wadded up my mother's silk áo dài and stored it for the past seventeen years. I notice that there are bugs all over the dress, I hear them buzzing. I am lured into a kind of trance. I put on the dress. In the kitchen, Grandmother Z grabs the white roses Mother had bought seventeen years ago and sticks them in my hair, and even though I don't expect it, I feel a massive relief to just disappear into someone else's stuff, to not make my own way anymore, to be, instead, led.

Upstairs in the room with paper flowers, Gorgeous stands dressed in her aunt's bridal costume. Kung Fu and Prof see her but don't touch her. They watch her hum the piano's hypnotic tune and walk away, revealing a book called *Lonely Days*.

Kung Fu tries to follow Gorgeous, but Gorgeous keeps disappearing. Maybe she's not even there, or moving between the sensible and material, the mirror and the door. Prof is stupefied: "It's unscientific, unexplainable, unnatural, unreasonable! *It doesn't make sense.*"

Kung Fu has already lost her faith, though. She's been led to another room, where she finds Sweet trapped inside the grandfather clock. Blood drips down the gears and teeth of the clock, behind the glass etched *HOUSE MADE*. Blood drips down the gears and teeth of the clock.

"I'm sorry, Sweet," whispers Kung Fu.

Entering the room, Prof is shocked and, finally, scared. "*How can such things happen in this world?*"

Daughter Grandmother Z and I lay in bed looking through a book of pictures of Dresden before it was bombed, completely leveled in World War II. She reads it to me like a children's book, narrating and then displaying the illustrations.

Grandmother Z Right here [*rubbing her finger across a page*]. I would get ice cream here with my Mami before the war. Oh, it was so lovely! It's gone [*she turns the page*]. Here was the market where we would go each morning. They called Dresden the Florence of the Elbe. It was *so elegant*. It's gone [*she turns the page*]. This is gone. When the bombs hit, I flew off my bicycle and hid in a ditch and watched my city become a torch. For years you would walk into the town center, everything rubble. Behind you, rubble, in front of you, rubble. The buildings looked like skeletons. This statue remained [*she rubs the image*], gazing at the heaps of stone.

Ach, when I touch the image, it is like I touch a part of me that's gone. Dresden is gone! My city is gone.

Daughter nervously pulls up the bed's blanket.

Daughter Grandmother, will you protect me when the war arrives? How will I know what to do?

Grandmother Z I might not even be here tomorrow. You will be on your own!

Daughter Grandmother, I'm scared.

Grandmother Z Oh good. *That*—that's where you will find your character.

Scene 2

Sister enters the room in a state of wonder. She stares up at the ceiling and twirls around and around, blowing smoke rings from her cigarette.

> *Sister* This room! I learned to walk in this room. Sister held me up and I couldn't wait to move. I was destined to go far in life. The memories! I must take a piece of the floor.

Sister takes a knife and begins to hack at a piece of the floor. Sister walks into the room and joins Sister. She copies Sister's smoke rings.

> *Sister* I started my period in this room! And mom was gone and I had no idea what to do so I just wadded up one of her magazines and stuck it in my vajoo. I need a piece of this room.

Sister takes a hammer, breaks off a part of the toilet lid, and sticks it up her vagina. Sister walks in the room and joins Sister. She, too, blows smoke rings.

> *Sister* I painted my first painting in this room. I locked myself in here for two weeks to paint, but in the end I spent the whole time watching detective shows and jerking off. Something about the madness of the girl detective, and all that music she thinks to, gets me every time. I guess I wanted to investigate what my clitoris was supposed to *do*!

Sister grabs a can of paint and dumps it on her head. It sticks to her like skin. Sister walks into the room and joins Sister. She lights her cigarette from the butt of Sister's cigarette and blows a smoke ring.

> *Sister* This room! I remember this room! I had my first broken heart in here. I cried and cried for a whole month straight.

Sister grabs a mop.

> *Sister* May this mop collect all my fallen tears.

Sister mops and whistles, a cigarette dangling out of her mouth. Sister walks into the room and joins Sister. She bums a cigarette.

> *Sister* [singing] Oh, back in thine old crypt! I remember! Khaos, I taught you how to get out of your crib in this room. I remember reaching my legs over the bar and letting it rub my conch. That was my first sexual experience. I can't help but marvel at how much I've grown. I need a piece of this room.

Sister grabs two pieces of wood and ties them to her feet like shoes. She does a jig. Sister walks into the room and lights up. Khaos coughs.

> *Sister* I remember this room! Let's reminisce! Khaos, I used to babysit you in here. You would copy every fucking thing I did. Mom never left any food in this house, just rice krispie treats, so I gave you my own petals for nourishment. I loved you as a child. You looked just like me and you loved rice krispie treats. I must take a piece of this room.

Sister grabs a hammer and bangs through the cabinet door. Bugs spill out of the holes in the cabinet. The sisters dance surrounded by the hazy light of smoke rings. Khaos takes a bite of her salad.

> *Khaos* You guys… I think my water just broke.
> *Sister* Oh my god.
> *Sister* What's the plan?
> *Khaos* I don't have one. Where's my foundation?
> *Sister* You never made a plan?
> *Sister* *[suddenly]* Baby room!
> *Sister* Do you have a baby room?
> *Sister* Paint it Hermès blue! You could call it the Hermès blue room.

The Sisters light up and smoke cigarettes dreamily, then one by one flick their cigarettes to the side. Grandmother V walks into the room surrounded by rings and auras, holding a giant box worth her body weight and wrapped in gold paper. She joins Grandmother Z and Daughter, who is still wearing the áo dài that is slowly being eaten by bugs, and seventeen-year-old flowers in her hair, in bed. Grandmother V sprays the flowers with formaldehyde to avoid further decay. Karma enters the room.

> *Khaos* Ugh, this is so suffocating. So many women, nowhere to go. It all reeks of formaldehyde.
> *Karma* Khaos! You were born into a dynasty of discussers. Think of this as a meeting of the *minds*.

Daughter pinches Grandmother V to confirm that she's real. Grandmother V pinches her back in the nipple.

Grandmother V Finally, you've grown some tooties. And a few other extra pounds.

Daughter Grandmother, I'm so sorry this áo dài is wrinkled. You see, no one has worn it in seventeen years. It's not even mine!

Grandmother V plumps her pillow.

Daughter Grandmother, I have so much to say to you.

There is a long pause.

Daughter Grandmother, I'm so sorry that I didn't recognize you when you first walked in. It's been many years and we've both changed. I am no longer a child.

Grandmother V moisturizes her face.

Daughter Grandmother, you always had such beautiful skin, even in the afterlife. I'm so sorry that I didn't visit your ashes at the temple. I was worried that my Vietnamese was not good enough to speak to the monks at the door.

Grandmother V brushes her long, dark hair.

Daughter Grandmother, I'm so sorry that I haven't spoken Vietnamese in seventeen years. I feel like I've thrown away a gift you gave me.

She is still brushing her hair.

> *Daughter* Grandmother, did you like the clothes you were wearing in your casket? I admit that I thought to myself that you wouldn't like them, your áo dài was a little bit garish. I'm sorry that I didn't scream and kick and demand that you depart in your favorite áo dài, looking almost Parisian!

Grandmother V turns on the TV.

> *Daughter* Grandmother, I'm sorry that when you were alive I only thought about you with babies. I'm sorry I didn't ask what you were like when you were young. Grandmother, were you a bad daughter too?

Grandmother V is absorbed in the TV. Daughter grips Grandmother V's arm.

> *Daughter* Grandmother! I'm so sorry that I'm wearing white!

There is no response. Daughter turns to the TV, too, where Prof and Kung Fu find Fantasy passed out next to Melody's chewed-up arm. They pick Fantasy up and she comes to, then looks away and passes out at the sight of the arm. They rush her to another room, carrying her like soldiers through a trench. "You were right. This is a haunted house!" they tell her. "We have to cooperate. It's the only way to survive!" Building a barricade against the door to the bedroom, Prof reads out loud from *Lonely Days*, as if by reading out loud she will break the spell: "There are no young girls in the village anymore. I'm all alone. But I'll keep waiting for him in this house. He wasn't killed in the war. I know he'll come back. Because he promised."

The light to the room begins to flicker. "Fantasy!" Gorgeous's voice whispers playfully. "I'm—I'm in my aunt's world!" Her face appears as large as a wall. "She died many years ago. She wanted to be married so badly that her body remained alive after her death. And she eats all the unmarried women who come here. That's the only time she can wear her bridal gown."

Daughter shakes the gold box Grandmother V brought with her into the room.

Daughter Grandmother, what's in the box?

There is no response. Daughter tears open the box.

Daughter I open the box and find a familiar smell, one that I haven't smelled in a very long time—the smell of her house. I dip my nose into the box and breathe deep, but then I realize it's just the smell of dust. Or was dust the smell of her house all along?

Grandmother Z So there's dust in the house. There's dust everywhere. Everywhere in the world. Even on a yacht in the middle of the ocean. There's still dust!

Daughter Where does it all come from?

Grandmother Z The moon!

The grandmothers explode into laughter. Daughter laughs too, because she does everything they do. They lay in bed watching TV, where, as if it were a tornado, the house lifts its things into the air. The center collapses: floorboards burst, walls break apart, glass shatters. The house swells and grows larger and larger until it takes the shape of a ghost. In a chorus of voices, the house says, "NOW IT'S YOUR TURN. JUST LET ME EAT YOU."

Khaos Guys, what does a contraction feel like?

Sister Like someone shoved an alien up your cervix and forgot to clip its talons!

Karma Khaos, get in the tub! You're gonna have to do a water birth!

Khaos wraps her blanket around her.

Khaos No way, mom! This water is disgusting. I look at what it does to the pots and I think about what it's going to do to my organs. Going up my throat, up to my cranium, down to my pituitary gland…

Karma I'll fix that water… add seaweed, antidepressants, CBD, lavender… and shea butter for stretch marks. Just get in the tub, Khaos. Mommy's right here with you and I've done this tons of times. Trust me. Get in the tub!

Khaos wraps her blanket around her and walks ever so slowly to the tub, her sisters holding her blanket like a bridal train, cigarettes hanging out of their mouths. When they get to the very end of their cigarettes, now long sticks of ash, they spit their butts onto the floor. Tiny embers skate gaily across the wood.

Meanwhile, on the screen, *House* ends with a formulaic "chase" or "swallow." Household objects fly around the rooms: mops, umbrellas, telephone wires, cushions. Shoes with no feet walk back and forth. Fantasy faints and is revived. Against colored backdrops, the girls take poses, part horror movie, part kung fu film, part fashion house. A door blows towards them and Kung Fu holds it as armor. The lamp swallows Kung Fu, and she disappears into a psychedelic world where body parts fragment into animated fields of flowers and skulls.

Back in the house, the floorboards break apart into rafts over a red river. Prof and Fantasy clutch each other as their raft shudders over the bloodbath.

"Mr. Togo!" Fantasy screams for their teacher who has promised he will come to rescue them. Prof finally loses her faith: "Maybe he isn't coming!" she says to Fantasy. "He didn't promise the house!" She loses her glasses and gets pulled into the water by a tin can with teeth—a *Jaws* joke. In the red water, her clothes fall off of her. She swims orgasmically and serenely, the outline of her red body fraying into blue like a digital ember. Fantasy floats alone on a raft.

Mr. Togo rolls into town with not-a-care-in-the-world. "Do you like watermelons?" asks the Farmer Selling Watermelons, stomping one, two, three times.

The stomp is a call to the gods. God is in the ground. Are you there, God?

"No!" says Mr. Togo.

The foot of the bed falls through the floor.

Scene 3

Daughter I grab the headboard frantically. What's going on? I say to my grandmothers. Is it the bugs? Is it the water? Is it the war?

Grandmother *Z* *[calmly]* Oh. This house needs a little maintenance. But it's all yours now.

Daughter Does it even work?

Grandmother *Z* If anyone can make it work, my daughter, it's you. You were born into a Dynasty of Survivors.

The toilet lid falls to pieces. A hole breaks into the wall. The window shatters. The fridge bursts. The wood splinters. Bugs march out from their kingdom in the wood. Chairs, curtains, bannisters, arches, sinks, clocks, chandeliers, and beer bottles fall to pieces. One thousand discarded cigarettes flare to become a fire, burning all the bed pillows, throw pillows, microfiber, and memory foam, forming a cloud of smoke, dust, quarters, and long, long strands of hair.

Daughter *[coughing]* What if toxic fumes blow in through the windows? What if it's too cold in here in the winter? How can I heat a house with holes? What about noise pollution? Light pollution? Traffic pollution? Tech pollution? Food pollution? What's to stop it from entering into my house? My skin? My bloodstream? My insides? I worry all day. I worry about my heart. I worry about it beating. Sometimes I worry that my worry spreads to my organs. I worry that I have no control over them. But they control me. Without them, I'm nothing!

I can really spook myself, grandmother! It's like a room I go into. But the problem is, sometimes I can't get out.

Grandmother *Z* I don't know about that room.

Daughter *[leaning her head on Grandmother V's shoulder]* Then tell me again about The Feeling, Grandmother. The one where your skin is peeling wallpaper?

Grandmother *Z* I don't know about The Feeling. I don't know these rooms. I don't know these walls. Sometimes I just wake up and feel some kind of way.

Daughter Forgive me, grandmother. I don't know any other way to tell it to you.

The apartment keeps falling to pieces. Pipes burst and water rushes in through the floorboards of the house. The bed floats on an empty sea, surrounded by a ring of fire. A basket of bread floats by. Red bikini. Incense and singing bowls. Doll. Screen. Skinny paperbacks. Many mangoes. Grandmother V flips through the channels. A woman and her friend smoke and get stoned in a bathroom.

"Here's to our fantastic beautiful lives!" they cheer into the mirror. They take a sip of champagne.

Daughter *[whispering]* Grandmother, my spine is so *freaky*. It's a bone cello. It remembers *everything*...

Suddenly the friend falls to the floor. "I can't do it!" she cries. "You put your neck on the line, you put your neck out there, and they just... chop it off!"

A woman from the future would go to the ends of the Earth if someone—anyone—asked her to. This is because the people around her have always found something disappointing about her. She's learned to deal with this by being soft, being easy, having less sharp edges, but over time this just buries her edges under the surface, making a woman who's slightly stunned, overwhelmed, scalloped in nerves. Pressured and cracking.

In the future of the future, everything begins to crack. The lights are turned on too high, the zoom-ins pulse, the rapid jump cuts are nonsensical. When she becomes a beautiful, compliant changeling complicit in her own self-erasure she laughs a wide-open laugh. She is so over the moon she begins to eat everything in sight.

"Darling, who cares, you don't have to do anything, you know. You can do nothing, you can stay here!" The woman sits on the bathroom floor and smokes her spliff.

"I'm not nothing," says the friend.

"No, you're not nothing," agrees the woman.

"No, I'm not nothing!" says the friend. "I know I'm not nothing, I'm not born to die, but I'm not…" She crawls towards the camera. "I'm not *out there!*"

A celebrity enters a hotel room in Dubai. The room, at $27,000 a night, is really a ten-room suite with marble walls, ceiling murals, floral bouquets the size of trees, individually monogrammed pillowcases, and hot towels upon entry. The bathtub overlooks a hotel-size aquarium, where schools of fish and a scuba diver, holding a WELCOME! sign, swim by. An enormous dining table is stacked with enough plates of baked goods and fresh fruits to feed, her friend declares, 900 people. She sits at the head of the table with her sunglasses on, eating and talking on her cell phone.

"I'm here to help! I'm here to help!" says the woman from the future.

"Sandra Bullock's missing," says the voice on the phone.

"Oh noooo!" she laughs heartily. "Did I eat *herrrrr?*"

"You know that moment when you're in a room," the woman says, "or you're on a plane, and you think someone's looking at you, but then you find that they're just asleep, and their head is flopped in your direction?"

The friend nods, distant.

The woman rolls over on the bathroom floor. "Well, I don't want my life to be like that—whole world asleep."

The woman and her friend, who, earlier that day, had cut each other up, break into a room with a long dining table piled with baked goods and liquor, enough to feed 900 people. They grab the food by the handful and eat it, then throw it at each other. Cake all over her face, the friend grabs the curtains off their rods and drapes them around her body, posing on top of the head of the table. "Fashion show," she declares.

The woman from the future puts her hand to her mouth. "I do feel full!" She considers her fullness. "Of LIFE!"

Khaos holds up a petulant flower.

> *Khaos* It's a girl! She's new and disgusting. I love her!
>
> *Karma* This is so important… this is the most important moment… this moment is of cataclysmic importance!
>
> *[crying]* Khaos, I'm so proud of you! I'm so excited to watch you become the mother you were destined to be.

As Karma sobs, the Sisters applaud ambivalently. They pass the baby around and hold her.

> *Sister* What shall we name the baby?
>
> *Sister* What shall we name the baby?
>
> *Sister* What shall we name the baby?
>
> *Sister* What shall we name the baby?
>
> *Sister* What shall we name the baby?
>
> *Karma* WHAT SHALL WE NAME THE BABY? What name is unlike any other? Is gorgeous? Able to consume the fullness of life? Wants it all? Is willing to risk everything to have it?

Khaos closes her eyes and imagines the most wild, rare, and radiant image of herself. Finally, she announces:

> *Khaos* Hillside.
> *Sister* Ugh.
> *Sister* Ugh. That's so disgusting.

Khaos touches the baby flower to her cheek.

> *Khaos* No way, Sisters. It's epic.

The fire begun by the discarded cigarettes is spreading throughout the house. Grandmother Z flips through the TV. Four young girls wake up in a bunker they call "the dollhouse," with no discernible exits to the outside, where each room is meticulously designed to appear like their rooms at home. A young woman sits in her cavernous room, with no entrance or exit, taking off her faces. Eight young women, each named Chanel, live in a sorority house where, to the song "Forever Young," they serve: severed head. Grandmother Z pauses on a roomful of flowers smoking cigarettes and playing Rummikub, with a little baby flower in a vase in the center of a table.

> *Sister* What do you think the world looks like to her?
> *Khaos* I don't want to talk about it with you guys.
> *Sister* Why—you don't believe in our Sisterhood?
> *Karma* Are you waiting for a happy ending?
> *Khaos* For chrissakes, mom, that's the most cliché thing I've ever heard you say in my entire life. No, I don't believe in happy endings. I don't believe in endings at all! Only beginnings. New beginnings!
> *Sister* *[smiling cruelly]* We can be scared together.

The ring of fire approaches the bed, but Grandmother Z and Grandmother V do not seem to notice, or care. Daughter squeezes in between them and clutches her blanket. The Sisters, hundreds of them now, gather around Karma and Khaos in a circle. Their presence is total and suffocating. Holding hands, they begin to chant:

> *Sisters* We can be scared together!
> We can be scared together!
> We can be scared together!
> We can be scared together!
> We can be scared together!
> We can be scared together!
> We can be scared together!

Grandmother Z turns up the volume to drown out the sound of the fire spreading throughout the house. We can be scared together! We can be scared together! We can be scared together! We can be scared together! drones on and on like a white noise. Gorgeous appears at the top of the stairs. Fantasy floats towards her. "Gorgeous!" she says. "Tell me it's not true. You aren't a ghost!" She reaches for her, tears open her dress.

Daughter counts to one million to calm herself. She tells herself that if her grandmothers aren't afraid, then she also doesn't need to be afraid. She focuses on the screen, where Fantasy is clutching Gorgeous, leaning her head on Gorgeous's shoulder, one tit exposed. Daughter wraps her arms around Grandmother V and Grandmother Z. Fantasy says, "I want to sleep... Mommy!"

Gorgeous wraps her in a ghostly embrace.

Fantasy is the last to survive.

It is unclear whether Fantasy dies.

Daughter The water is calm and the light is blue like pale Downy detergent. After a few minutes, or a few years, Grandmother V starts telling me about life in Vietnam, before she had children. 'I'm telling you stories,' she says, which is a weird translation, the word means something between gossip and stories, 'so that when I leave this time you will not forget where you came from.' I am confused; my vocabulary in Vietnamese has to do with life in the house, specifically her house, and the kinds of things that we used to talk about. I keep asking her to explain the words that she is using, but I don't always understand the words she uses when she explains them. 'I gave you my voice when you died,' I try to express to her. 'Please give it back to me. We will both feel better, I'm sure of it.' But she looks confused, so I bring up my fears about the apartment and its holes, the things that are falling apart, and she says to me, 'A [   ] can be used to put it together,' but I don't understand the first part of the sentence, and the second part has an untranslatable word that means real togetherness, like not the togetherness of things, but the togetherness of people: not two people side by side, but two people joined. I think she might be telling me how to fix this house through a concept I don't understand in her language, an adult concept. She keeps on telling me stories that I don't understand, and I pretend to fall asleep, out of embarrassment, sadness, and frustration: For so long I have wanted to talk to her again and now she's here and I don't understand a thing she's saying. I feel I am a broken link. I think that one day my children will not speak this language, will not grow up in a house where Vietnam is so close and ever-present, and if it is preserved at all for the next generation it will be something like a flower pressed into the pages of an old book, cuing the person who, when they might spend a day here or there thinking about the past, will open it up and fill in the environment that surrounds the flower, wondering about what made it bloom and what made it suffer, what were its shades in the morning light, sketching but never knowing, like I have with my mother, and she did with her mother, and her grandmother, except that, beginning with my generation, the environment and the thing preserved were always just out of reach. My grandmother had died and taken all the things she saw with her eyes with her, and there is no way in hell to get any of it back. I pretend to sleep until she just whispers and then turns to watch more TV. The water rocks us calmly on its surface. Blue light covers itself on my forehead and seeps until I am filled with the blue of water, Downy detergent, and screen light, filtering through the spot on my forehead I had touched to my grandmother's when she was dying, and to the ground when my grandmother died. My immortal forehead.

I hear the fire continue its slow burn as we lay there floating on my mother's bed. At one point, I am certain I burned, too. When I hear my grandmothers' gentle snoring, I open my eyes to take a look at the room around me. The furniture, the walls, the trash can, everything is burned but still in its shape intact. When I touch it, it turns to ash.

APPENDIX TO RULES OF STYLE AND
ANATOMY OF A CRITICAL INCIDENT

As chronicled in "Rules of Style," an unwieldy constellation of sources was consulted throughout *Fantasy*'s research process. I wish to acknowledge those sources that were quoted directly:

Atkinson, Michael. "Rediscovering the Japanese Horror Flick *House*." *The Village Voice*, 12 Jan. 2010, https://www.villagevoice.com/2010/01/12/rediscovering-the-japanese-horror-flick-house.

Haden, Courtney. "Dreams in the Wind." *Weld*, 12 May 2015, [URL no longer active].

Dargis, Manohla. "Watch Out for That Disembodied Head, Girls." *The New York Times*, 15 Jan. 2010, p. C7.

Hagen, Kate. "31 Days of Feminist Horror Films: *House*." *The Black List Blog*, 27 Oct. 2017, https://blog.blcklst.com/31-days-of-feminist-horror-films-house-8a35dcfe87a5.

"*House*." *The Criterion Collection*, https://www.criterion.com/films/27523-house.

Kennedy, Rory. *Last Days in Vietnam*, PBS, 2014.

Kogonada, "Trick or Truth." http://kogonada.com/portfolio/trick-or-truth.

McCabe, Taryn. "Why *Hausu* Remains One of the Weirdest Horror Films Ever Made." *Little White Lies*, 17 Sept. 2017, https://lwlies.com/articles/hausu-weirdest-horror-film-ever-made.

Neil, Chuck. "I'm Dreaming of a White Christmas." *Tears Before the Rain: An Oral History of the Fall of South Vietnam*, Oxford University Press, 1990, pp. 198–200.

Obayashi, Nobuhiko. "Making of Dreams: A Movie Conversation Between Akira Kurosawa and Nobuhiko Obayashi." *Dreams*, The Criterion Collection, 1990. DVD.

O'Keeffe, Christopher. "Yubari 2014 Exclusive Interview: *House* Director Obayashi Nobuhiko Talks *Seven Weeks* and the Art of Cinema." *ScreenAnarchy*, 17 Mar.

2014, https://screenanarchy.com/2014/03/yubari-2014-exclusive-interview-house-director-obayashi-nobuhiko-talks-seven-weeks-and-the-art-of-ci.html.

Raine, Michael. "Adaptation as 'Transcultural Mimesis' in Japanese Cinema." *The Oxford Handbook of Japanese Cinema*, edited by Daisuke Miyao, Oxford University Press, 2014, pp. 101-123.

Rosenfield, Esther. "50 Queer Writers, 50 Favorite Queer Films." *Pastemagazine.com*, 26 June 2019, https://www.pastemagazine.com/articles/2019/06/50-queer-writers-50-favorite-queer-films.html.

Schreiber, P., and J. Schreiber. "Diagnosis and Prevention of Operator Error and Equipment Failure." *Seminars in Anesthesia*, VIII, no. 2, June 1989, pp. 141–148.

Simon, Noah. "Dollar Cinema Screens Cult Classic '*Hausu*'." *The McGill Tribune*, 6 Nov. 2018, http://www.mcgilltribune.com/a-e/dollar-cinema-screens-hausu-06112018.

Tobias, Scott. "*House*." *AV Club*, 28 Oct. 2010, https://film.avclub.com/house-1798222306.

Wada-Marciano, Mitsuyo. "Imaging Modern Girls in the Japanese Woman's Film." *Nippon Modern: Japanese Cinema of the 1920s and 1930s*, University of Hawai'i Press, 2008, pp. 76–129.

Walkow, Marc. "Constructing a House." *House* (1977), The Criterion Collection, 2010. DVD.

APPENDIX TO THE MATERNAL ECOLOGY

Mother, Daughter, Grandmother Z, Grandmother V, Karma, Khaos, and Sisters lived in a house steeped in scenes from the following films, TV shows, music and YouTube videos: *House, Valerie and Her Week of Wonders, Keeping Up with the Kardashians, Mekong Hotel, Grey Gardens, 3 Women, Picnic at Hanging Rock, Heavenly Creatures, Daisies, Mulholland Drive, To Our Daughter, Lady Dynamite, Absolutely Fabulous, Pretty Little Liars, No Tears Left To Cry*, and *Scream Queens*.

ACKNOWLEDGMENTS

Thank you: first and foremost, to Sidebrow, for your commitment to emergent forms, and for investing in a young, unknown writer. *Fantasy* is a book about homes: Thank you for giving it one and for loving it, for allowing it to be wild and wayward, for understanding its idiosyncrasies and arguments and guiding it to be the best it can be, patiently as the book transformed from one draft to the next, far different than the one that was originally submitted to you. I was, I still am, awed and honored to be among this group of writers.

To Jack Jones Literary Arts, most especially Kima Jones and Frank Johnson, for this incredible dream of an audience.

And to Sojourner Truth Parsons, for your image "She's Still Crying!," which has wrapped *Fantasy* in its glow.

To Donald Breckenridge for publishing excerpts from an earlier draft of *Fantasy* in *The Brooklyn Rail*, and to the editors of *glitterMOB*, *littletell*, *Emergency Index Vol. 5*, and *The Stockholm Review of Literature*, who published pieces that were cannibalized in Fantasy, too. The curators and programmers of DAMA, SPF15, BWSMX, Cool Breeze TV, the Museum of Contemporary Art San Diego, Now That's What I Call Poetry!, and A Ship in the Woods offered me multidisciplinary platforms and magnificent stages that let my words move across forms and bodies. And also, the readers of the 2017 Nightboat Poetry Prize selected this book, in an earlier iteration, as a finalist. I was emboldened by all of these opportunities and accomplishments.

A whole draft of *Fantasy* was revised at LMCC's *Workspace* residency and I am forever indebted to LMCC, especially Bora Kim and Alessandra Gomez, for hooking me up with a studio with river views, a community of artists that I came to call friends, and readers whose insight pushed me to transform *Fantasy* in new and exciting ways.

This book frankly wouldn't have been possible had academic fellowships not granted me intellectual and financial support and fantastic healthcare. I owe deep gratitude to the Screen Cultures program at Northwestern University, especially Ariel Rogers, and the Writing Department at UC San Diego, especially Brandon Som, Anna Joy Springer, Erin Suzuki, Ben and Sandra Doller, Rae Armantrout, Amy Adler, and Alain J.-J. Cohen, in whose graduate seminar I presented on "the recurrence of the disfigured face in *House*." Thank you Laurie Weeks for being a life-changing first writing teacher, and also, thank you Christina Mesa, for your guidance and friendship over so many years: I don't remember the person I was when I first stepped into your office, but thank god she found you.

To my friends who form my closest creative community, who have shaped my evolving artistic avatar and its secret inner self, thanks for lifting me up when I was spiralling down, for making me feel that I am still near: Ellen Schafer, Terttu Uibopuu, Pablo Dodero, Maria Rios-Mathiodakis, Angella d'Avignon, Catherine Czacki, Ash Eliza Smith, and Corrine Fitzpatrick. Lev Kalman and Whitney Horn, our overlapping ghost story has allowed me to vampirically, vicariously live in your practice. And of course, my kindred cozy girl, Paola Capó-García: You taught me about screens that grieve and are always one step ahead of me, showing me the way.

To my family: For your support and sustenance and all that cannot be named, but which I have nevertheless tried to name, thank you.

And to the Eros to my Rose, Morgan Mandalay: You put plants in my studio so that I'd be happy writing in it. The creation of this book was set against an ambient backbeat of such daily gestures of care for my work, my peace of mind, my heart, and my intellect. You are my home. Even when we're off the island, *we can be scared together.*

Kim-Anh Schreiber is author of the plays *Kult of Konsciousness* and *Meatloaf.* Her multidisciplinary work has been published and exhibited in outlets such as *The Brooklyn Rail*, *littletell*, *Emergency Index*, *BWSMX*, the Museum of Contemporary Art San Diego, and elsewhere, and has been supported by the Lower Manhattan Cultural Council (LMCC) and the New York Center for Book Arts. She has appeared in the film *Two Plains & A Fancy*, and the forthcoming projects *Lone Pair, Dream Team*, and *Candy Ego*, a sci-fi noir comedy written in collaboration with Ash Eliza Smith. She received her MFA in Writing from UC San Diego and is a PhD student in the Screen Cultures program at Northwestern University. *Fantasy* is her first book.

ADVANCE PRAISE

"The semi-autobiographical fantastic *Fantasy* of Kim-Anh Schreiber is rooted 1/4 in Vietnamese/Germanic realism and ancestral context, 1/2 in Nobuhiko Obayashi's 1977 *House*, 1/4 in matriarchal estrangement, and 0% bikini-clad pool party. Schreiber uses the fabric of cinema and horror to quasi-measure the length and width of her pre-adolescent and adolescent consciousness. It's a GORGEOUS dress that the ghost in her psyche demands that it wears before falling into ash. Here, in these immolatable, scriptive dialogues with all of her consanguineous, anecdotal, exegetical selves ('who become shoes without feet that walk back and forth' in a house that eats like hungry ghosts), her psyche is cut, recut, uncut, though not forgotten, un-linearly and nonchalantly and numerously, by her relationship to film and her relationship with her Vietnamese mother, surrogated mother in grandmother(s) and auntie(s). Through the art of disfigurement/defacement, her intimate rapport to pain and her sacral joint, and her friendship with abandonment, she is able to elevate her daughterly North Star duties to subliminal heights. As Kim-Anh Schreiber seeks closure with the uncloseable, we see an acutely talented scholar and inventive memoirist on her way to becoming more than Sandra Bullock's neighbor." **—Vi Khi Nao**

"'Every seam I encountered in the fabric of my reality was like a disfigurement that someone had smoothed over and left silent,' writes Kim-Anh Schreiber in this remarkable investigation of female anger and resilience, intergenerational trauma, and what might be called the development of literacy in the subject of pain. Schreiber, the daughter of a Vietnamese refugee and a German immigrant, combines recognizable modes — memoir, criticism, dramatic play script — into something as uncategorizable as the film she deploys throughout the book as muse and foil: Nobuhiko Obayashi's 1977 post-Hiroshima 'horror-comedy' *House*, in which generations of women are trapped together in a haunted house. Beginning with extended considerations of the instability of memory ('an evocative curator'), of the 'impossible problem of drawing a picture,' and of the pull to use projection and doubling as bridges across gaps in experience and understanding, *Fantasy* finally resolves into a flickering, unstable but vivid portrait of a mother and daughter both separated and bonded by history, violence, human fallibility, and love." **—Anna Moschovakis**